SURRENDER/SUBMISSION
BOUND HEARTS 1 & 2

Surrender/Submission
Bound Hearts 1 & 2

Lora Leigh

Copyright © 2017 by Lora Leigh

To give the heart, love in its most powerful form, is the greatest surrender of all…

– Lora Leigh

Chapter One

"Tess, you coming to my party?" It was her father's voice on her answering machine that finally roused her from sleep. "You better be here, girl. I'm tired of you staying away. You call me back."

The line disconnected. Tess sighed as she opened her eyes. She would have preferred the dream to the stark loneliness that awaited her when she opened her eyes. At least there, even in the dark, frightening abyss of desires too dark to name, she had a purpose, rather than her fears.

She stared down at the large stuffed gorilla she clutched to her chest in her sleep. A present from her father when she left with her mother. Something to keep the bad dreams away, he had said sadly, even though she had been an adult. Tess often had bad dreams.

Perhaps she shouldn't have left as well, Tess often thought. She was just entering college at the time, and could have made her own choice. But her mother had needed her. Or Tess had thought she did. Now she wasn't certain if her mother needed her, or merely needed to control her.

"Tess, you awake now?" Her mother, Ella James, called from the bottom of the downstairs hallway, her voice barely penetrating the distance.

Tess had installed her own phone line straight out of college and moved her bedroom to the upper floor where her mother rarely ventured. She needed her privacy, and her mother was prone to butt in wherever she could. The stairs kept her from venturing into Tess's privacy very often.

"Yeah, Mom. I'm awake," she yelled back, rising from bed, imagining her mother's moue of distaste. It was Saturday, for God's sake. She was entitled to sleep in. She could just imagine her mother's expression if she knew it was her father's call that woke her.

Resigned, Tess got of bed and headed for the shower.

Tess was well aware of her mother's disgust for her father's lifestyle. Jason Delacourte didn't stay home or keep regular hours or play the nine to five game. He owned a national electronics corporation and lived the lifestyle he chose. He gave dinners, attended charities and threw yearly parties. Ella preferred her books and her quiet and anything that didn't involve a man. She had done her best to raise her daughter the same way.

Tess did hate parties. She always had and she knew she always would. She invariably ended up going alone. Always ended up leaving alone. Parties jinxed her. Men jinxed her, they had for years. But she was committed to this party. She'd promised. What could she do but get ready to go?

She grimaced, confused as she pondered her lack of a love life. Or perhaps sex life. She wasn't a great believer in love or the happily ever after stuff. She had rarely seen it work; her own parents were an example of that one. And her father's second marriage seemed more rocky than solid.

She frowned as she usually did when she thought of her father's new wife. Well, perhaps not new. Jason Delacourte, her father, had been married for nearly three years now to Melissa. The woman still insisted that everyone call her Missy. As though she were still a teenager. Tess snarled with distaste. Of course, the woman was barely thirty-five, ten years younger than her father, and nearly ten years older than Tess. The least he could have done, she sniped silently, was marry a woman closer to his own age.

She could barely tolerate being in the same room with 'Missy'. The woman gave dumb blonde a new meaning. How she managed to be related to a man touted as a genius, Tess had no idea.

Cole Andrews was Missy's brother, and Tess's father swore Cole had moved Delacourte Electronics into the financial sphere it now enjoyed as one of the leading electronic manufacturers.

The thought of him caused mixed reactions in Tess, though.

Cole was six feet three inches of hard packed muscle and dark, brooding good looks with a cynical, mocking attitude that drove her crazy. His kisses were the stuff dreams were made of. His fingers were wicked instruments of torturous pleasure; his lips were capable of throwing her into a hypnotic trance when they touched her.

She suppressed a sigh. No man kissed as good as Cole Andrews. It should be a crime that one man should ooze so much sex appeal, and be such an asshole to boot. And it was really a crime that she couldn't get past that one stolen kiss long enough to enjoy any others.

After showering, she quickly blow-dried her hair, sighing as she swiped the brush through her shoulder-length black locks one last time before turning back to the open doors of her large closet.

She had enough clothes. One thing her father had always done was made certain she was well provided for. Elementary school teachers didn't make a lot in terms of money, and it wasn't the glamorous job Jason Delacourte had always thought his daughter should hold, but it was what she wanted to do. Besides, it kept her out of the social sphere her stepmother and Cole Andrews moved in. That was a big enough plus to keep her there.

But, she had promised her father she would stay with him for this one week. That she would take the time off work and return to the large family home she had grown up in before his divorce from her mother, and she would try to be his daughter.

It wasn't that she didn't love him, she thought as she packed her suitcase. She did. She loved her father terribly, but Cole was at the house. He stayed there often, and it was Cole she needed to avoid.

After packing the more casual clothes she would need and her treasured, hidden vibrator, Tess moved back to her closet to choose what she would wear for the yearly Valentine's Day party her father gave. It was also the third anniversary of his marriage to Missy. Yeah, she really wanted to celebrate that one.

She pulled a short, black, silk sheath from the closet and hung it on the doorknob. From her dresser she pulled out a black thong, a lacy matching bra, and smoky silk stockings. The dark colors suited her mood. Valentine's Day was for lovers, and Tess didn't have one. She still didn't understand why she was going to this stupid party.

It wasn't like her father would really miss her. The house would be packed. They didn't need her there. She hadn't attended one of Missy's parties in well over a year now. They were loud, bustling, and often turned out a bit too wild for her tastes. Besides, Cole always ended up bringing his latest flame, and pissing her off the first hour into it.

His dark blue eyes would watch her, faintly cynical, always glittering with interest while the bimbos at his side simpered adoringly. She snorted. If she had to simper to hold him, well then—

She sighed desolately. She would probably simper if she thought it would help. If she could learn how. Her mouth always seemed to get the better of her, though. His general air of superiority just grated on her. Ever since that first kiss, when his hard body held her captive against the wall as he whispered what he wanted in her ear. Her body had sung in agreement; her mind, shocked and dazed from the images, had kicked in with an instant defense: her smart mouth.

It had been over two years.

She sat down on the bed, still naked, her cunt wet, throbbing at the memory.

"Can you take the heat, baby?" he had whispered to her, holding her against the wall as he ground his cock between her thighs. "I won't lie to you, Tess. I want you bad. But I'm not one of your little college boys that you can mess with. I want you tied to my bed, screaming, begging for me. I want to pump my dick in your tight little ass. I want to hear your cries while I'm buried there and fuck you with a dildo bought just for that tight pussy of yours."

She shook now in remembered arousal and hot desperate need. "Sure," she had bit out. "And then I can fuck your ass next!"

He had had the nerve to laugh at her. Laugh at her as his fingers sank into the wet, tight grip of her pussy and her orgasm rippled over her body. She'd gasped, feeling the slick heat as it pulsed through her vagina, washing over his fingers. Then he had slid them down to the tight little hole he had promised to fuck, one finger sinking in to its first knuckle, sending a flare of pain through her body that she had enjoyed too much to be comfortable with.

Tess remembered her fear, throbbing as hot as her lust. She had pushed him away, trembling, unfamiliar with the hot pulse of hunger that had flared in her, unlike anything she had known before. And he had watched her, his cock a thick, hard outline beneath his pants, his eyes dark as she stood before him trembling.

"Pervert!" she had said accusingly.

His lips had quirked, his eyes flaring in anger.

"And you?" he asked her. "What does that make you, baby? Because sooner or later, you'll have to admit you want it."

"What, rape?" she had bit out.

His eyes suddenly softened, a strange smile quirking his lips.

"Never rape, Tess. You'll beg me for it. Because we both know you want it as much as I do. My cock sliding up your tight ass while you scream for me to stop, then screaming for me to never stop. You're mine, Tess, and I know what it takes to give you what you need. When you're ready to accept that, let me know."

Tess shook her head. Wanting it and accepting it were two different things. She had dreamed of it ever since, too humiliated to ask him for it, and he refused to offer a second time.

She touched her smooth, waxed pussy, her eyes closing as she lay back on the bed. The thought of what he wanted terrified her, yet it aroused her to the point of pain. The thought of his cock, so thick and hard, easing into her ass as he penetrated her wet, pleading cunt with a dildo, her tied down, unable to fight, unable to escape whatever he desired, had her soaked with need. He wouldn't hurt her. She knew enough about Cole to know he would never hurt her, but he could show her things she wasn't sure she was ready to know about herself. He could show her a part of herself that she wasn't certain she could handle. That was a frightening thought.

Her fingers eased through the shallow, narrow crease of her sex, circled her clit. He had promised to eat her there. To run his tongue around her clit, suck it, eat her like honey, a lick at a time. She shuddered, moaning, imagining her finger was his tongue, licking at her cunt, lapping at the slick heat that soaked her pussy. She circled her clit, whispering his name, then moved her fingers back down to the desperate ache in her vagina. She penetrated the tight channel with two fingers, biting her lip, wondering how thick and long Cole's fingers would be inside her. He had such big hands, he would fill her, make her scream for more.

He had whispered the dark promise that he would fuck her ass, take her there, make her scream for him. She bit her lips, her fingers moving, one inserting into that tiny, dark hole while she wished she hadn't packed her vibrator so quickly. As her finger passed the tight entrance, she allowed two fingers of her other hand to sink into her vagina. She could hear his voice in the back of her mind, feel his finger, thicker than hers, spearing a dart of pleasurable pain through her as he pierced her ass. And he had told her, warned her he would fuck her there.

Her knees bent, her hips thrusting harder against her own fingers as she imagined Cole between her thighs, licking her, fucking her with his fingers, driving her over the edge as they fucked into her; her cunt, her ass, until—

She cried out as the soft ripples of release washed over her. Her vagina clenched on her fingers, her womb trembling with pleasure. It wasn't the release she had experienced with Cole's fingers or her vibrator, but it took the edge off the lust that seemed to only grow each time she saw him.

Each time she looked into his knowing, far too hungry gaze. And she wondered how much longer she could hold out against those hungers.

Chapter Two

It wasn't enough. An hour and a cold shower later, Tess's body still simmered with need. Stretched on her bed, her body sheened with sweat as she fought for orgasm, she cursed the phone when it rang at her side. Grimacing when it refused to stop, Tess reached over, grabbing the receiver.

"Hello." She tried to clear her throat, to still her rapid breaths, and hoped she could explain it away if it was her father. She didn't want him to know his daughter was a raging mass of horny hormones ready to explode.

There was a brief silence, as though the caller were weighing his words.

"Feeling better?" A trace of knowing mockery, a deep, sensually husky voice whispered the words.

Tess flushed at Cole's voice. Damn him.

"I haven't been sick," she bit out, her eyes closing as her vagina pulsed. She smoothed her fingers over her clit, feeling the increased stimulation there. Damn, she could get off with just his voice.

"No, just trying to get off," he said lazily. "I'd help. All you have to do is ask." *Ask, ask,* her inner voice begged.

"In your dreams." She winced as the words burst from her mouth. Damn him, he put her on the defensive faster than anyone she knew.

"It would appear in yours as well," he said, his mockery suddenly gone. "I know how you sound when you're aroused, Tess. Don't try to lie to me. Let me hear you. Touch yourself for me."

Tess felt her breath strangle in her throat.

"You're a pervert, Cole." She fought for her own control at the sound of that sexy voice. "Isn't phone sex illegal?"

"I'm sure most of what I want to do with you could be termed illegal," he chuckled. "Let's talk about it, Tess. Come on, tell me what you were doing to yourself. Are you using your fingers or a vibrator?"

"I do not have a vibrator." She clenched her teeth over the lie.

"Dildo?" he whispered the words heatedly. "Are you fucking yourself, Tess? Thinking about me, how much I want you?"

"No!" She clenched the receiver in her hand, shaking her head despite the fact that her fingers had returned to her suddenly pulsing cunt.

"I'd like to see you in my bed, Tess, your legs spread, your hands touching your pretty pussy, fucking yourself. Did I ever tell you I bought that dildo I promised you? It's nice and thick, Tess. Almost as large as my cock. I want to watch you use it. See you fuck yourself with it."

"God, Cole," she gasped. "We're on the phone. This is indecent." But her fingers were sinking into her sex again.

"What were you doing before I called, Tess?" His voice was dark, hot. "I know you were touching yourself. I know the sound of your voice when you're ready to come, and you're ready to come, baby. I hear it."

"No—" She tried to deny the obvious truth, but she couldn't keep her breath from catching as her fingers grazed her clit once again.

"Son of a bitch, Tess," he growled. "Are you close, baby?" His voice deepened. "If I were there, I'd make you scream for it. I'd fuck you so deep and hard you wouldn't be able to stop it. You'd come for me, Tess. Come for me now, baby. Let me hear you."

His voice was so deep, so sensual and aroused it caused her womb to contract almost painfully. Her body bowed, her breath catching on a near sob. He brought all her darkest desires, her deepest fantasies, to the forefront of her mind. It terrified her.

"Cole." She whispered his name, wanting to deny him, but her fingers weren't listening as they stroked her clit, sank into her vagina, then moved back to repeat the action.

She was so hot she could barely stand it. So horny she was on the verge of screaming for relief.

"I'm stroking my cock, Tess, listening to you saying my name, imagining you touching your juicy cunt, wishing I were with you, watching you fuck yourself with the dildo I bought you." His words caused her to gasp, her womb to contract painfully, her hips to surge into her plunging fingers.

"No." She tossed her head. She couldn't do this.

"Damn, Tess, I want to fuck you," he growled, his voice rough. "I want to be buried so deep and hard inside you you'll never forget it or deny me again. Come for me, damn you. At least let me hear what I can't have. Fuck yourself Tess, give this to me. Those aren't your fingers buried in your pussy, it's my cock. Mine, and I'm going to fuck you until you scream."

Tess's orgasm ripped through her. She shuddered, whimpered, her body tightening to the point of pain before she felt her vagina explode.

"Oh God, Cole," she cried, then heard his hard exclamation of pleasure, knew he was coming, knew her climax had triggered his own as well.

"Tess," he groaned. "Damn you, when I get hold of you I'll fuck you until you can't walk."

Tess trembled at the erotic promise in his voice, the dark sensuality that terrified her, made her want to give him whatever he wanted.

"No," she whispered, fighting for breath, fighting for sanity. "I asked you to stay away."

She wanted to whimper, she wanted to beg. There was silence over the line.

"Stay away?" he asked her carefully. "I don't think so, baby. I've stayed away too long as it is. You're mine, Tess, and I'm going to prove it to you. All mine. In every way mine, and I'll be damned if I'll let you deny it any longer."

Chapter Three

Her mother was waiting for her when she came down the stairs, her suitcase in hand. Ella Delacourte was a small, spare woman, with dark brown hair and sharp hazel eyes. There were few things she missed, and even fewer that she was tolerant of.

"So, you're still going," she snapped out as she eyed the suitcase Tess set by the front door. "I thought you would have more pride than that, Tess."

Tess pressed her lips together as she fought to keep her sarcastic reply in check.

"This has nothing to do with pride, Mother," she told her quietly. "He's still my father."

"The same father who destroyed your family. Who ensured you lost the home you were raised in," Ella reminded her bitterly. "The same father that married the whore who meant more to him than you did."

Tess's chest clenched with pain, and with anger. She wasn't a child anymore, and there were times when she could clearly see why her father had been unable to get along with her mother. Ella saw only one view, and that was hers.

"He took care of us, Mother," she pointed out. "Even after the divorce."

"As though he had a choice." Ella crossed her arms over her breasts as she stared at Tess in anger.

"Yes, Mother, he had a choice after I reached eighteen," Tess reminded her bleakly. "But I believe he still sends you money and provides whatever you need, just as he does me. He doesn't have to do this."

"Conscience money," Ella spat out, her pretty face twisting into lines of anger and bitter fury. "He knows he did us wrong, Tess. He threw us out—"

"No, you elected to leave, if I remember correctly." Tess wanted to scream in frustration.

The argument never ended. It was never over. She felt as though she continually paid for her father's choices because her mother had no way of making him pay.

"He's depraved. As though you need to spend a week in his house." Ella was shaking now with fury, contempt lacing each word out of her mouth. "Those parties he throws are excuses for orgies, and that wife of his—"

"I don't want to hear it, Mother—"

"You think your father and his new family are so respectable and kind," she sneered. "You think I don't know how you watched that brother of hers. That I didn't know about the flowers he sent you last year. They're monsters, Tess." She pointed a thin, accusing finger at Tess. "Depraved and conscienceless. He'll turn you into a tramp."

Tess felt her face flame. She had fought for years to hide her attraction to Cole. She had heard all the rumors, knew his sexual exploits were often gossiped about. He had more or less admitted them to her on several occasions.

"No one can turn me into a tramp, Mother," she bit out. "Just as there's no way you can change the fact that I have a father. I can't ignore him or pretend he doesn't exist, and I don't want to."

Tess faced her mother, feeling the same, horrible fear that always filled her at the thought of making her too angry. Of disappointing her in any way. But as she faced her fear, she felt her own anger festering inside her. For so many years she had tried to make up for the divorce her father had somehow forced. She knew he took the blame for it. Just as her mother vowed complete innocence. She was beginning to wonder if either of them would ever tell her the truth.

"You'll end up just like him," Ella accused, her eyes narrowing angrily. Tess could only shake her head.

"I'll be home in a week, Mother," she said, picking up her luggage.

In the back of her mind, she knew she wouldn't be returning, though. She had stayed out of guilt and out of fear of failing somehow in her mother's eyes. She was only now realizing she could never succeed in her mother's opinion. She was fighting a losing battle. A battle she didn't want to win to begin with.

Tess was still trembling when she pulled into the large circular driveway of her father's home. The evening shadows were washing over his stately Virginia mansion, spilling long shadows over the three-story house and the tree-shrouded yard. The drive from New York wasn't a hard one, but her nervousness left her feeling exhausted. She definitely wasn't up to facing Cole. Her face flushed at the thought. She had tried not to think about the phone call that morning, or the core of heat it had left lingering inside her.

It had nearly been enough to have her turning around several times and heading back to her safe, comfortable life in her mother's home. She would have, too, until she thought of her mother. Ella was too frightened of the world to draw her head out of her books and see the things she was missing. She had lost her husband years before their divorce because of her distaste of his sexual demands. She told Tess often how disgusting, how shameful she found sex to be.

Tess didn't want to grow old knowing she had passed up the exciting things in life. She didn't want to ache all her life for the one thing she needed the most and passed up. But she didn't want her heart broken. And Tess had a feeling Cole could break her heart.

She wanted him too badly. She had realized that in the past months. The dreams were driving her crazy. Dreams of Cole tying her to his bed, teasing her, touching her, his dark voice whispering his sexual promises to her. She was awaking more and more often, her cunt soaked, her breathing ragged, a plea on her lips.

Tess had known he was bad news even before her father married his sister. His eyes were too wicked, his looks too sensual. He was wickedly sexy, sinfully sensuous. She moaned in rising excitement and fear.

Leaving her keys in the ignition for the butler to park it, Tess jumped from the car. Night was already rolling in, and she would be damned if she would sit out in that car because she was too scared to walk into the house. Hopefully, Cole wouldn't be there. He wasn't always there.

"Good evening, Miss Delacourte." The butler, a large, burly ex-bouncer, opened the door for her as she stepped up to it.

Thomas was well over fifty, Tess knew, but he didn't look a day over thirty-five. He was six feet tall, heavily muscled and sported a crooked nose and several small scars on his broad face. He'd told her he was Irish, with a mix of Cherokee Indian and German ancestry. His thick, brown hair was in a crew cut, his large face was creased with a smile.

"Good evening, Thomas. Is Father in?" She stepped into the house, more uncomfortable than she had thought she would be.

This was the home she had grown up in, the one she had raced through with the puppy her father had once bought her, but her mother had gotten rid of. The home where her father had once patched skinned knees and a bruised heart. The home her mother had taken her out of when her father demanded his rights as a husband, or a divorce.

"Your father and Mrs. Delacourte are out for the evening, Miss," he told her as she stepped into the house. "Will you be staying for a while?"

"Yes." She took a deep breath. "My luggage is outside. Is my room still available?"

There was an edge of pain as she asked the question. She had learned that Missy had opened her room for guests, rather than keeping it up for Tess's infrequent returns.

"I'm sorry, Miss Tess," Thomas said softly. "The room is being redecorated. But the turret room is available. I prepared it myself this morning."

The turret room was the furthest away from the guest or family bedrooms. At the back of the house, on the third floor. The turret had been added decades ago by her grandfather and she had loved it as a child. Now she resented the fact that it was not a family room, but the one she knew Missy used for those visitors she could barely tolerate. Evidently, Tess thought, she had slipped a few notches in her stepmother's graces.

Tess breathed in deeply. Those weren't tears clogging her throat, she assured herself. Her chest was tight from exhaustion, not pain.

"Fine." She swallowed tightly. "Could you have my luggage brought up? I need a shower and some sleep. I'll see Father in the morning."

"Of course, Miss Tess." Thomas's voice was gentle. He had been with the family for as long as she could remember and she knew she wasn't hiding her pain from him.

"Is Father happy, Thomas?" she asked before going down the hall to the hidden staircase that led to the turret room. "Does Missy take care of him?"

"Your father seems very happy to me, Miss Tess," Thomas assured her. "Happier than I've seen since Mrs. Ella left."

Tess nodded abruptly. That was all that mattered. She moved quickly down the hall, turning toward the kitchen then entering the staircase to the right. The staircase led to one place: the turret room.

It was a beautiful room. Rounded and spacious, with furniture that had been made to fit. The bed was large with a heavy, rounded walnut headboard that sat perfectly against the wall. Matching drawers slid into the stone wall for a dresser, with a mantel above it to the side of the bed. Across the room was a small fireplace. It used gas logs, but it was pretty enough.

She felt like Cinderella before the Prince rescued her. Tess sat down heavily on the quilt that covered the bed. This sucked. She should get back in her car and head straight back home. She didn't belong here anymore, and she was beginning to wonder if she ever had.

Taking a deep breath, she ran her hands through her hair and listened to Thomas coming up the stairs.

He stepped into the room with a friendly smile, but his brown eyes were somber as they met hers.

"Will you be okay here, Miss Tess?" he asked as he set the large suitcase and matching overnight bag on the luggage rack beside the door. "I could quickly freshen another room."

She shook her head. "No. I'm fine, Thomas." What was the point? She had come back, mainly to find something that didn't exist. It was best she learn that now, before it went any further.

Thomas nodded before going to the fireplace. With practiced moves he lit the fire, then pulled back and nodded in satisfaction at the even heat coming off the ceramic logs.

"Would you like me to announce dinner for you, Miss Tess?" he asked.

Her father and stepmother were away. Tess knew the servants would only be preparing their own food. She shook her head. They were all most likely anticipating a night to relax, and she wouldn't deprive them of that. What hurt the most was her father's absence. He had known she was coming, and he wasn't here. It was the first time he had ever left, knowing she was coming home. The first time Tess had ever felt as though she were a stranger in her own home.

One thing Tess really liked about the turret room was the bathroom. The huge room was situated to the right of the bed, and held a large sunken tub big enough for three and a fully mirrored wall. Thomas had stocked the small refrigerator unit against her objections. One of his little surprises was a bottle of her favorite white wine. Tess opened it, poured a full glass and sipped at it as the water ran into the large ceramic tub. Steam rose around the room, creating an ethereal effect with the glow of the candles she had lit.

She stripped out of her jeans and T-shirt and setting the wineglass and bottle on a small shelf, sank into the bubbling liquid. Exquisite. She leaned back against the hand-fashioned back of the tub and rested her head on the pillowed headrest. It was hedonistic. A wicked, sinful extravagance, as her mother would have said.

She closed her eyes and took a deep breath. She had expected her father to be home, had expected some sort of greeting. She didn't expect to be left on her own. But the sinful richness of the bathtub eased a bit of the hurt. She could enjoy this. This one last time.

She hadn't come home without ulterior motives, she knew. Perhaps this was her payment for it. It wasn't her father that had drawn her so much as the man that she knew would arrive sooner or later.

Cole.

She took a deep breath, flushing once again at the memory of the phone conversation. She could handle a little sex with him. It wasn't like she was a virgin. It was the rest of it. Cole didn't go for just sex.

Cole was wild and kinky and liked to spice things up, she had heard. She whimpered, remembering his promise to tie her to his bed and what he would do there.

She had never had rough sex; though, she admitted, she had never had satisfying sex either. It had never been intense enough, strong enough. The hardest climax of her life had been in that damned hallway, with Cole's fingers thrusting inside her cunt. She had been so slick, so wet, that even her thighs had been coated with it.

Lifting the wineglass from the shelf, Tess sipped at it a bit greedily. Her skin was sensitive, her breasts swollen with arousal, her cunt clenching in need. Dammit, she should have found a nice, tame principal or teacher to satisfy her lusts with. Cole was bad news. She knew he was bad news. Had always known it.

She had known Cole before her father had married his sister. She had heard about his sexual practices, his pleasures. He was hedonistic, wicked. And sometimes, he liked to dominate. He wasn't a bully outside the bedroom. Confident, superior, but not a bully. But she had heard rumors. Tales of Cole's preferences, his insistence on submission from his women. The comments he had made to her over the years only backed up the rumors.

Tess trembled at the thought of being dominated by Cole. Equal parts fear and excitement thrummed through her veins, her cunt, swelling her breasts, making her nipples hard. She didn't need this. Didn't need the desire for him that she was feeling.

Didn't need the broken heart she knew he could deal her. She drained the wine from her glass then poured another, realizing the effects of the drink were already beginning to travel through her system. She felt more relaxed, finally. She hadn't been this relaxed in months. Enjoying the sensations, she poured another, hoping she would at least manage a few hours of sleep tonight without dreaming of Cole.

Chapter Four

Tess came downstairs the next morning expecting to be greeted by her father. She had dressed in the dove gray sweater dress he had sent her the month before. Tiny pearl buttons closed it from the hem to just above her breasts. On her feet she wore matching pumps, and there were pearls at her neck. Confident and sure of herself, Tess felt able to field her father's questions, his urgings that she move back home for a while. But when she walked into the dimly lit family room, it was Cole she found instead.

She stood still, silent, as she faced him across the room. His eyes, brilliant blue and filled with wicked secrets, watched her narrowly. Thick, black lashes framed the dark orbs, just as his thick, black hair framed the savage features of his face. His cheekbones were high, sharp, his nose an arrogant slash down his face. His lips were wide, and could be full and sensual or thin with anger. Now, he seemed merely curious.

His arms were crossed over his wide, muscular chest, his ankles were crossed as he stood propped against the back of a sectional couch that faced away from her.

"Where's Father?" Tess asked, fighting her excitement, her own unruly desires.

"He was held up. He expects, perhaps, to be home tomorrow," he told her quietly. "Perhaps?" She barely stilled the tremble in her voice.

"Perhaps." He straightened from his lazy stance, watching her with a narrow-eyed intensity that had her breasts and her vagina throbbing. Damn him for the effect he had on her.

"He couldn't tell me himself?" she asked nervously, watching him advance on her, determined to stand her ground.

"I'm sure he'll call, eventually." His voice was a slow, lazy drawl, thick with tension and arousal. It was all she could do to keep her eyes on his face, rather than allowing them to lower to see how thick the bulge in his pants had grown. She knew for certain the throb in her vagina had intensified.

"So, you volunteered as the welcome wagon?" She was breathless, and knew he could hear it in her voice. His eyes darkened with the knowledge, causing her heartbeat to intensify.

He moved steadily nearer, until he was only inches from her. She could feel the warmth of his body, and it tingled over her nerve endings. He was tall, so much broader than she. She felt at once threatened and secure. The alternating emotions had her caught, unable to move, unwilling to run.

The blood raced through her veins as she attempted to make sense of the powerful feelings racing through her body and her mind. For two years she had thought about him, fought the temptation he represented and the heat he inspired.

"I'm always here to welcome you, Tess." He smiled, that slow quirk of his lips that made the muscles in her stomach tighten. "But I have to admit, I was more than eager after talking to you yesterday."

Her face flamed. Echoes of her whimpers, her fight to breathe through her climax, whispered through her mind. Cole's voice, husky and deep, urging her on, rough from his own arousal, then his own climax.

Tess swallowed hard as she caught her lip between her teeth in nervous indecision. Did she reach out for him? Should she run from him?

"Hound dog," she muttered, more angry at herself than she was at him. He chuckled, his hand reaching out to touch the bare flesh at her neck.

"Prickly as ever, I see," he said with a vein of amusement as his eyes darkened. "Would you be as hot in bed, Tess?"

"Like I would tell you!" she bit out.

She fought the instinct to lean closer to him, to inhale the spicy scent of aroused, determined male.

"Hmm, maybe you would show me," he suggested, his voice silky smooth, heated.

Tess trembled at the low, seductive quality of his voice. It traveled through her body, tightening her cunt, making her breasts swell, the nipples bead in anticipation. Her entire body felt flushed, hot. Then the breath became trapped in her throat. His hand moved, the backs of his fingers caressing a trail of fire to the upper mounds of her heaving breasts.

He looked into her eyes, his own slumberous now, heavy lidded. "Mine," he whispered.

Her eyes widened at the possessive note in his voice.

"I don't think so." She wanted to wince at the raspy, rough quality of her voice. "I belong to no man, Cole. Least of all you."

So why was her body screaming out in denial? She could feel the bare lips of her cunt moistening as her body prepared itself for his possession. Her skin tingled, her mouth watered at the thought of his kiss.

"All mine," he growled as a single button slid free of its fragile mooring over her heaving breasts. "You knew there was no way I would stay away after hearing you climax to the sound of my voice, Tess. You knew I wouldn't let you go."

She shrugged, fighting for her composure, an independence that seemed more ingrained than needed at the moment.

"You don't have a choice but to let me go," she informed him, feeling trepidation dart through her at the sudden intensity in his eyes.

His fingers stroked over the rounded curve of her breast, his expression thoughtful as he stared down at her.

"Why are you fighting me, Tess?" he suddenly asked her softly. "For two years I've done everything but tie you down and make you admit to wanting me. And I know you do. So why are you fighting it?"

"Maybe I want to be tied down and forced to admit it," she said flippantly, ignoring the flare of excitement in her vagina at the thought. She had heard the rumors, knew the accusations her mother had heaped on her father's brother-in-law for years. "Yeah, Cole, me tied down, just waiting for you and one of your best buds. Hey hon, the possibilities are limitless here."

Her mouth was the bane of her existence. She mentally rolled her eyes at the sharp, mocking declaration.

"My best buds, huh?" He tilted his head, watching her with a slight smile.

"The more the merrier." She moved away from him, denying herself the touch she wanted above all others. "You know how it is. A girl has to have some kind of excitement in her life. May as well go all the way."

Tess was going to cut out her own tongue. She felt more possessed than in possession of any common sense. Tempting Cole, pushing him, was never a good idea. She knew that from experience. Yet it seemed she knew how to do little else.

"Tess, be careful what you wish for." He was openly laughing at her. "Have you ever had two men at once, baby?"

The endearment, softly spoken in that dark, wicked voice sent her pulse racing harder than before.

"Does it matter?" She turned back to him, some demonic imp urging her to tease, to tempt in return.

She flashed him a look from beneath her lashes, touching at his hips, suppressing her groan at the size of the erection beneath his jeans. Damn, he was going to bust the zipper any minute now.

"Doesn't matter." He crossed his arms over his chest. "I can give you whatever you want, Sugar. If you really want it. I'm flexible."

Cole felt his dick throb. Damn her, he knew she had no idea how far she truly was pushing him. He could see the excitement in her eyes, a glimmer of sexual heat, of determination. Did she think she could turn him off by giving him carte blanche to do his worst? She had no idea how sexual he could get. The thought of tying her down, forcing her to admit the needs of her body, or his needs, was nearly more than his self-control could bear. The thought of introducing her to the pleasures of a ménage, hearing her screams of pleasure echo in his ears, had his cock so hard it was a physical ache.

He wanted Tess to have every touch, every sexual experience she could ever imagine wanting to try. He wanted her hot, wet, and begging for his cock. He wanted her to admit to her needs, just as he finally admitted to his own. He wanted Tess, now, tomorrow, forever. However he could get her, every way she would let him have her.

Cole watched the flush that mounted her cheekbones, the flare of interest in her eyes that she quickly doused. She thought it a game, a sexual repartee that she could easily brush aside later. But it didn't change the fact that Tess had given such ideas more than a passing thought. He could see it in the hard rise and fall of her breasts, the swollen curve of them, the hard points of her nipples. They were nearly as hard as his cock.

She couldn't know, he thought with a thread of amusement, just how much he would enjoy doing both things with her. The dominance level he possessed was incredibly high. Introducing her to being tied down, teased, tormented, or sandwiching her between his body and Jesse's—

He had to forcibly tamp down his lust. Not that sharing her would be easy, or would happen often, but there was a particular pleasure in it that could be found in no other sexual act. The thought of total control of her body, her desires and her lusts was an aphrodisiac nearly impossible to resist.

"Tess, you shouldn't dare me," he warned her carefully. "You don't know what you could be asking for, baby."

He felt honor bound to give her one chance, and one chance only, to still the raging desires building inside him. She didn't know, couldn't know, the sexuality that was so much a part of him. A sexuality and dark desire he had been willing to dampen for her. But her bold declaration that she could handle them was more than he could resist.

"Maybe I do know." He loved the breathless quality in her voice, the edge of fear and lust in her voice was a heady combination.

"I would fuck your ass, Tess," he growled advancing on her once again. "Is that what you want? My best bud sinking in that tight pussy while I push inside your back hole. You would scream, baby."

The idea of it was making him so hot he could barely stand the heat himself.

"Hmm..." Her pink lips pouted into a moue of thoughtfulness. "Sounds interesting, Cole. But you know, I couldn't allow just anyone such privileges." She sighed regretfully. "Sorry, darling, but it appears you're out of luck."

Oh, she was in trouble. Cole kept his expression only slightly amused, allowing his sweet Tess to dig her own grave.

"And what qualities must a man have to be so lucky?" he asked her as he deliberately maneuvered her against the wall, his body pressing against hers, not forcing her, but holding her, warming her.

For a moment, an endearing vulnerability flashed in her eyes. His heart softened at what he read there. Mingled hope and need, a flash of uncertainty.

"Something you don't have." He wondered if she heard the regret in her voice.

"And what would that be, baby?" He wanted to pull her to his chest, hold her, assure her that anything she needed, anything she wanted, was hers for the asking.

She pushed away from him, her natural defensiveness taking over again, that flash of pain in her eyes overriding her need to play, to tease and tempt.

"Heart, Cole. It takes a heart," she bit out. "And I really don't think you have one."

❧ ❧ ❧

Tess walked away quickly, anger enveloping her. It did little to tamp down the desire or the raging cauldron of emotions that threatened to swamp her. Damn. Double damn. She couldn't love him. She couldn't need his love. Two years of sparring with him, of fighting his advances and his heated looks, couldn't have caused this.

She felt her body trembling, her chest tightening with tears. Loving Cole was hopeless. She didn't stand a chance against the sophisticated, experienced women he often slept with. She had seen them, hated them. Knowing he took them to his bed, made them scream for his touch, was more than she could bear. Surely, she didn't love him. But Tess had a very bad feeling she did.

Chapter Five

Tess came awake hours later, a sense of being watched, studied, breaking through the erotic dream of Cole teasing her, tempting her with a kiss that never came. On the verge of screaming out for it, the presence in her room began to make itself known.

She blinked her eyes open, frowning at the soft light of a candle on the small half-moon table by her bed. Her head turned, her heart began to race. Cole was sitting on the side of the bed watching her, his blue eyes narrowed, his muscular chest bare except for the light covering of black hair that angled down his stomach and disappeared into—Her eyes widened, then flew back to his. He was naked. Sweet God, he was naked and sporting a hard-on that terrified her. Thick and long, the head purpled, the flesh heavily veined.

Tess was suddenly more than aware of her nakedness beneath the heavy quilt. When she had gone to bed, she had thought nothing of it. Now she could feel her breasts swelling, her nipples hardening. Between her legs, she felt the slow, heated moistening of her fevered flesh. She felt something else, too. Her arms were tied to the curved headboard, stretched out, the same as her legs, with very little play in the rope. Son of a bitch, he had tied her on her bed like some damned virginal sacrifice.

"What have you done?" She cleared the drowsiness from her voice as he sat still, watching her with those wicked, sensually charged eyes. "Untie me, Cole. What are you doing here?"

"First lesson," he told her, his voice soft as his lips quirked in a sexy grin. "Are you ready for it?"

"Lesson?" She shook her head, her voice filled with her surging anger. How dare the son of a bitch tie her up? "What the hell are you talking about?"

His hand lifted. Tess thought he would touch her, grab her. Instead, those long fingers wrapped around his cock absently, stroking it. She swallowed tightly, her mouth watering, aching to feel that bulging head in it. She may have even considered giving into the impulse, if she could have moved her body.

"Your first lesson in being my woman, Tess," he told her, his voice cool, determined. "I told you I was tired of waiting on you. Tonight, your first lesson begins."

Tess rolled her eyes as she breathed out in irritation.

"Are you a secret psycho or something, Cole?" she bit out. "Did you just pay attention to what you said? Now let me go and stop acting so weird. Dammit, if you wanted to fuck, you should have just said so."

He smiled at her. The bastard just smiled that slow, wicked grin of his.

"But, Tess, I don't want to just fuck," he said, his voice amused. "I want you know who controls your body, your lusts. I want you to know, all the way to your soul, who owns that pretty pussy, that tempting little ass and hot mouth. I want you to admit they're mine, and mine alone to fuck however I please."

Damn. She knew Cole was into kink, but rape?

"Cole." She fought to keep her voice reasonable. "This is no way to go about getting a woman, hon. Really. You know, flowers, courtship, that's the way to a woman's heart."

"Really?" He was openly laughing at her now. "I sent you flowers, darling—" Her eyes widened.

"Oh yeah, with a card telling me what size butt plug to buy so you could fuck my ass," she bit out as she jerked at the ropes binding her ankles. "Real romantic, Cole."

She remembered her sense of horror, the shameful excitement when she read the card. She had dumped flowers and all in the trash, but kept the card. Why, she wasn't certain.

He shrugged easily. "Practical," he told her. "I wanted you prepared. But since you were unwilling to prepare yourself, then you'll just have to accept the pain."

Pain? No. No pain.

"Now look, Cole," she warned him reasonably. "Father will be really pissed with you. And you know I'll tell—"

"I asked your father's permission first, Tess," he told her softly, his expression patient now. "Why do you think your mother finally left your father? She refused to accept who he was and what he needed. I will not make that mistake with you. You will know, and you will accept to your soul, your needs as well as my own. You won't run from me. Your father understands this, and he's giving me the time I need to help you understand."

Tess stared up at Cole, fury welling inside her as her arms jerked at the ropes that held her. Damn him, they weren't tight, but there wasn't a chance she could smack that damned superior expression off his face.

"You're lying to me," she accused him. "Father would never let you hurt me."

"Ask him in the morning." He shrugged lazily. "You'll be free by then."

A sense of impotency filled her. Damn him, he thought he had all the damned answers and all the damned plans. She wasn't a toy for him to play with, and she would show him that.

"I'll have you arrested," she promised him. "I swear, if it's the last thing I do I'll have you locked up."

He was quiet for long moments, his eyes glittering with lust, with cool knowledge.

"I wouldn't do that if I were you. And I think come morning, perhaps you will have changed your mind."

Tess breathed in hard, watching him with a sense of fear, and hating the arousal that it brought her.

"What are you talking about?" she bit out.

His hand ceased the lazy stroking of his cock, then moved to her stomach. Her muscles clenched involuntarily at the heat and calloused roughness of his flesh.

"Tonight, I'll give you a taste of what's coming," he promised her. "You'll learn, Tess, who your master is, slowly. A step at a time. Nothing too hard, baby, I promise."

Tess shivered. He didn't sound cruel, but he was determined. His voice was soft, immeasurably gentle, but filled with purpose. He would have her now, and he would have her on his terms.

"This isn't what I want, Cole," she said, fighting for breath, for a sense of control.

His hand moved lazily from her stomach, his eyes tracking each move, his fingers trailing between her thighs until one ran through the thick, slick cream that proved her words false. She trembled, biting back a moan of pleasure as the thick length of his finger dipped into her vagina.

"Isn't it?" he whispered. "I think you're lying, Tess. You shouldn't lie to me, baby."

Before Tess knew what was coming, his hand moved, then the flat of his palm delivered a stinging blow to the bare folds.

Tess jerked at the heat. "You son of a bitch," she screamed, jerking against her bonds, ignoring the lash of pleasure that made her clit swell further. "I'll kick your ass when I get out of here."

Cole grinned, then moved from her side to position himself between her spread thighs.

"Let me go, you bastard!" she bit out, fighting to ignore the shameful pleasure and anticipation rising inside her.

"Naughty Tess," he whispered, his hand smoothing over her cunt, sliding over the moisture that laid thick and heavy on her pussy lips. "You're tight, Tess. How long has it been since you had a lover?"

"Kiss my ass!" she cried out, then jerked in surprise as his palm landed on the upper curve of her intimate flesh. She fought the ropes, terrified of the shocking vibrations of pleasure in her clit that radiated from the heat of the blow. "Damn you!"

Her body arched as his finger slid inside her vagina once again. It was a slow stroke, the hard digit separating her muscles, making the flesh tremble in building ecstasy. She fought the need to whimper, to beg at the slow penetration.

"How long, Tess, since you've had a lover?" he asked her again.

Tess realized she was panting now, primed, ready to climax. God, if he would just let her get off.

"I hate you," she growled.

His finger stopped. Halfway inside her, her muscles clenching desperately in need, and he stopped.

"You aren't being nice, Tess," he whispered. "I could leave you tied here, hot and hurting for relief, or I could give you what you need, eventually. Now, answer my question. How long?"

The threat was clear. His finger was still inside her as he watched her, his expression hard now, though his eyes retained that lazy, gentle humor. The contrast was almost frightening.

"Four years. Satisfied—Oh God!" Her back arched, her head digging into the pillows as his finger slid home with a smooth, forceful plunge.

Tess was shuddering, her climax so close she could feel herself pulsing in desperation.

"Damn you're tight." His fingertip curved, stroking the sensitive depths as she writhed against her bonds. "As tight as a virgin. I bet your ass is even tighter."

Tess stilled, quivering, seeing the lust, the excitement filling Cole's face. His cock was huge, thick and long, and she knew it would stretch her until she was screaming for relief. But her ass? No way. From the look on Cole's face though, he had figured out the way of it.

Chapter Six

"Cole, let's be reasonable," Tess panted, her vagina clenching around the finger lodged inside it, quivering from the deep, gentle strokes his fingertip was administering. "Your cock won't fit there. Stop trying to scare me."

But she had a feeling it wasn't an idle threat.

He smiled. She knew better than to trust that smile. It was a slow curve of his lips, a crinkle at the corners of his eyes. Watching her carefully, he slid his finger from the soaked depths of her hot channel and then moved to lie down beside her.

Tess watched him carefully, like he was a wild beast, as he propped his head on his arm and watched her through narrowed eyes. Then his gaze shifted, angling to her thighs, her eyes following as his hand moved.

"No—" she cried out helplessly as his hand raised.

She jerked. His head moved, his lips latching on to a hard, pointed nipple a second before he delivered another stinging blow to the wet inner lips.

She cried out, pleasure and pain dragging a helpless sound of confused desire from her lips as her body bowed and she jerked against him. His tongue rasped her nipple as he suckled her, and the next blow was delivered to the flesh that shielded her swollen clit. Her cry was louder, her body jerking, arching, fighting both pain and pleasure as she struggled to separate the two. She was on fire, her mind reeling from the confusing morass of sensations. She wanted to beg for more, beg for mercy.

Another blow struck her, his palm angled to deliver the blow from her clit to her vagina as he pinched her nipple between his teeth. The stinging pain, hot and fierce, had her clit throbbing as she screamed from a near climax.

"Please," she begged, her head thrashing against the pillow as she felt his arm rise again. "Please, Cole—"

A strangled scream left her throat as the hardest blow landed, striking with force and fire, sending her clit blazing, her orgasm peaking against her will. It shuddered through her body as his palm ground into her clit with just enough pressure to trigger her release.

Then his lips covered hers with a groan, his tongue spearing into her mouth with greed and hunger. Tess fought to get closer, her arms and legs protesting their confinement as she met his kiss with equal voraciousness, her tongue tangling with his, her moans a harsh rasp against her throat as she felt her cunt throb, her vagina ache for more.

Tess shuddered with the throbbing intensity of her climax, a distant part of her was shocked, amazed that she could respond in such a way. Fiery tingles of sensation coursed over her body, licked at her womb, left her greedy, hungry for more. Her cunt was empty, a gnawing ache of arousal tormenting it now. It wasn't enough. She needed more. So much more.

"Do you need more, Tess?" he growled as he pulled back and stared down at her. His eyes were no longer patient, they were hot and hungry, watching her intently.

"More. Please, Cole. I need you," she moaned. She stared up at him as her body moved restlessly, needing him, wanting his cock until she could barely breathe, her arousal was so intense.

He moved back, his hand going between her thighs, a ravenous groan coming from his throat as he felt the thick layer of cream that now coated her flesh.

"Your pussy's so hot, Tess." His voice sounded tortured. "So hot and sweet, I could make a meal of you now."

"Yes." She twisted against him, needing him to touch her, to fuck her, to relieve the yawning pit of exquisite need throbbing inside her.

"Not yet," he denied her, making her whimper. "Not yet, baby. But soon. Real soon."

She watched as he moved from her, going to his knees then propping her pillows beneath her shoulders and head.

"You know what I want, Tess," he told her, his voice rough, his cock aiming for her lips. "Open your mouth, baby, give me what I want."

Anything. Anything to convince him to relieve the ache that throbbed clear to her stomach. Her lips opened, and she moaned as the thick head pushed past them, stretching them wider. He was huge, so long and thick she wanted to cry out in fear, scream at him to hurry and fuck her with it.

"Oh yeah, such a hot little mouth," he groaned, wrapping his fingers around the base as he penetrated her mouth, stopping only when her eyes began to widen with the fear he would choke her. "Relax your throat, Tess," he urged her. "Just one more inch, baby. Take one more inch for me and I'll show you how good I can make you feel next."

Her pussy throbbed out her answer. *Yes, take more, bitch. Take it all so he'll fuck me.* The ravenous creature that was her pussy demanded her obedience as fiercely as Cole did. Breathing through her nose, her eyes on his, she slowly relaxed the muscles of her throat, feeling him by slow increments give her the final inch he demanded she take.

His hand tightened on his cock, his fingers brushing her mouth as he marked her limit, and still there was so much more. He pulled back as Tess suckled the thick length, her tongue washing over it, rasping the underside of his dick as he nearly pulled free of her mouth until she was slurping on nothing but the engorged head, and loving it.

Then he began to penetrate again. A slow measured thrust that sank his cock to the depth he marked, his expression tightening with such extreme pleasure that she fought to caress the broad head that attempted to choke her. She let her throat make a swallowing motion, a tentative movement to test her ability to do it.

⚜ ⚜ ⚜

Cole groaned, his dick jerking in her mouth as he pulled back, thrust home again. She repeated the movement, watching his face, never letting go of his expression as he began to fuck her mouth. He was panting, his teeth clenched, his hard stomach tighter now.

"Yes, swallow it," he growled when she repeated the motion. "Swallow it, baby. Show me you want my cock."

He was fucking her mouth harder now, and her lips were stretched so wide they felt bruised, but Tess loved the feeling, loved watching the excitement, the extreme lust that crossed his face each time her throat caressed the head of his cock. His hips were bucking against her, his voice was a rumbled growl as he fucked her, pushing his cock as deep as it could go, groaning as the flesh tensed, tightened further.

"Yes. I'm going to come now, Tess. I'm going to come in your hot little mouth just like I'm going to come up that tight little ass. Take it, baby, take my cock." He speared in, she swallowed, his hips jerked, then Tess felt the first hard, hot blast of his semen rocket against the back of her throat. It was followed by more. Thick hard pulses of creamy cum spurted down her throat as he cried out above her.

Tess was ecstatic, quivering with anticipation as she felt his cock, still hard, pull from her mouth. He would fuck her now. Surely, he would fuck her now.

"You're so beautiful, Tess," he whispered as he moved away from her, staring down at her, his eyes gentle once again. "So damned hot and beautiful, you make me crazy."

"Good," she moaned. "Fuck me now, Cole. Please." He smiled, and her eyes widened as he shook his head.

"What?" she bit out, incredulously. "Damn you, Cole, you can't leave me like this."

"Did I say I was leaving you?" he asked her, arching his brow in question. "No, Tess, I'll be here with you, all night, every night. But you're not ready to be fucked yet."

"I promise I am," she bit out. "I really am, Cole." If she got any more ready, she would go up in flames.

He chuckled, though the sound was strained. "Not yet, Tess," he whispered. "But soon."

He moved across the room, and then Tess noticed the small tray that sat on the mantel of her wall-enclosed dresser. He picked it up and as he turned back to her, Tess's eyes widened in apprehension.

There were several sexual aids on the silver tray, as well as a large tube of lubrication. The one that frightened her most was the thick butt plug that sat on its wide base. Tess trembled at the sight of it, shaking her head in fear as he neared her. If only she was frightened enough, she thought distantly. God help her, her cunt was on fire, her body so sensitive she thought a soft breeze would send her into climax. And seeing those toys, the thick butt plug and the large dildo, had her trembling, not just in fear, but in excitement.

He set the tray on her nightstand, then sat on her bed, staring at it.

"If you don't stay aroused, needing me and what I'll give you, then I'll walk away," he said, his voice so soft she had to strain to hear it. "But I'll push you, Tess, see what you like, see what you can take. Not just tonight, but all week. You're mine until the night of your father's party. No matter what, no matter when, as long as what I'm doing arouses you."

"And if it doesn't?" she asked angrily. "What are you going to do, hurt me until I can't take it anymore?"

He turned to her, his eyes blazing.

"Only I can give you what you want, what you need," he bit out. "You're so damned hot to be dominated you can't stand it. Do you think I don't know that? Did you think you were told the rumors of my preferences needlessly? If you weren't excited by it, Tess, you wouldn't have been so wet you soaked my hand two years ago when I caught you in the hall. You're just scared of it. And I want you too damned bad to let you stay frightened of what we both need any longer."

"I won't do it!" But excitement was electrifying her body, making every cell throb in anticipation.

"Won't you?" he growled. "I know about the books your mother found in your room when you went to college, Tess. The stories you read, to satisfy that craving you couldn't explain."

Her face flushed. Her mother had been enraged over the naughty books she had found in Tess's room that year.

"Captives, dominated by their lovers. Submissive, loving every stroke of the sensual pleasure they received."

Tess could feel the flush of mortification staining her entire body.

"Did you ever fuck your ass, Tess?" he asked her softly, leaning toward her, watching her closely. "As you stroked your cunt, fighting for orgasm, did your finger ever steal into that hot, dark little passage, just to see what it felt like?"

She had. Tess moaned in humiliation. But it hadn't been her finger, rather it had been the rounded, slender vibrator she kept hidden. The dark surge of pleasure that had spread through her had been terrifying. Even worse had been the hard, shocking quake of an orgasm that had her nearly screaming, ripping through her body, making her vagina gush its slick, sticky fluid. The remembered pain of the penetration, the humiliation of that rushing liquid squirting from her, had caused her to never try such a thing again except with her fingers. Even now, two years later, the thought of that one act was enough to leave her flushing with shame.

"Did it hurt, Tess?" And of course, those wicked eyes knew the flush of admission on her skin. "Did it make you want more?"

"No," she bit out, shaking with nerves, with arousal.

"I think it did." He touched her cheek, his fingers caressing her flesh, his voice gentle. "I think I left you aching, needing, and too damned scared to try to reach for it. I think, Tess, that you need me just as much as I need you."

"And I think you're crazy," she bit out, refusing him, wondering why she was when she needed it so damned bad.

His thumb stroked over her swollen lips, his eyes dark, glittering in the light of the candle.

"Am I?" he asked her softly. "Let's see, Tess, just how crazy I am."

Chapter Seven

Tess watched Cole, trying to still the hard, rough breaths that shook her body. She couldn't seem to get enough oxygen, couldn't seem to settle the hard shudder of her pounding heart.

"There's a fine line that divides pleasure and pain," he told her as he removed the butt plug and the tube of lubricant from the tray. "It's so slim, that if gone about the right way, the pain adds to the pleasure, in a dark erotic manner."

He moved to the bottom of the bed. He loosened the ropes attached to the footboard, then grabbed her legs quickly before she could kick out at him. Ignoring her struggles and heated curses, within minutes he had her entire body flipped over, the ropes once again holding her in position as he tucked several pillows beneath her hips.

"You bastard." Her voice was strangled as crazed excitement shot through her body.

Her buttocks were arched to him now. She was spread, open to him, and the flares of fear and excitement traveling through her body had her shuddering with arousal.

"God, Tess, you're beautiful," he growled from behind her, his voice rough, filled with lust. "Your little ass so pink and pretty. And I like how you keep your pussy waxed so soft and smooth. But I would have preferred to do it myself. From now on, I'll take care of it for you."

Tess trembled, crying out. She should hate this. She should be screaming, begging him to stop; instead her body pulsed in need and desire, in anticipation.

"You shouldn't have waited so long to come back, Tess," he whispered as he kissed one full cheek of her ass. "You shouldn't have made me wait so long, baby, because I won't be able to be as gentle as I would have been."

Her inner flesh pulsed at his words.

"And I'll have to punish you." She whimpered at the rising excitement in his voice. "But I would have anyway, Tess. Because I need to see that pretty ass all red and hot from my hand."

"No—" Despite her instinctive cry, his hand fell to the rounded cheek of her ass.

Heat flared across her flesh, then she screamed as his finger sank into her pussy a second later. She twisted, writhed against her bonds.

"You're so wet," he groaned. "So tight and hot, Tess. But by the time my cock sinks into your pretty pussy, you'll be tighter."

His hand struck again as the broad finger retreated from her quaking vagina. As the heat built in the flesh of her buttocks, his finger sank in again.

Tess was crying out a wash of dark, erotic excitement. The blows weren't cruel, rather sharp and stinging, building a steady heat in her flesh.

"So pretty." He whacked the other side, then his finger thrust into her again.

She was so wet she was dripping. He alternated mild and stinging blows that kept her flinching in anticipation. Kept her flesh heated, the pain flaring through her body. A pain she hated, hated because the pleasure from it was driving her crazy. She could feel her juices rolling from her sex, hear her cries echoing with needs she didn't want to name.

By the time he finished, her ass felt on fire, her hips were rolling, her vagina throbbing. She was dying of need. If he didn't fuck her soon, she would go crazy. She was burning, inside and out, a wave of fiery lust tormenting her loins as she fought the depraved pleasures of the spanking.

"Your ass is so pretty and red now," he groaned. "Damn, Tess, I like you like this, baby, all tied up for me, reddening, your cunt hot and tight and so wet it soaks my fingers." Two fingers plunged inside her.

"Cole—" Her cry was hoarse and desperate as she teetered on the edge of orgasm.

"I'm going to put this plug up your ass now, Tess," he warned her as he drew his fingers from her body. "Then I'll fuck you, baby. I'll fuck you so deep and hard you won't ever leave me again."

Tess's head ground into her pillow as his hand separated her buttocks. She flinched at the feel of cold lubricant, then cried out again as his finger sank fully into the tight hole. It pinched, sent a flare of heat through her muscles that had her bucking into the thrust.

"Oh, Tess, your ass is so tight." He twisted his finger inside her, spreading the lubrication, stretching the muscles as she whimpered in distress. "It doesn't want to stretch, baby. Such a pretty virgin hole."

As full as his finger filled her, how would she ever take more? She tightened on him in fear, then moaned as the heated pain made her inner flesh throb hotter. She was depraved. She should be terrified, fighting him, instead her whimpers were begging for more.

He repeated the lubrication several times as Tess fought to breathe past the pleasure and pain. She was ready to scream, to plead. She wanted to whisper the forbidden words. She bit her lip, panted, cried out as his finger finally withdrew.

"Tess, I want you to take a deep breath," he finally instructed her heatedly. "Relax when the plug starts in, it will ease the pain if it's too much for you at first."

"You're torturing me," she cried out, bucking against her ropes. She didn't want this now. She was too scared. The dark lust rolling over her was too intense, too frightening. "Stop, Cole. Let me go!"

"It's okay, Tess." His hand smoothed over her bottom, then his fingers clenched, separating her again. "It's okay, baby. It's normal to be scared. Just relax."

"Cole—" She didn't know if her cry was in protest or in need as she felt the tapered head of the thick plug nestle against her tiny hole.

"It's going to hurt, Tess." His voice was dark, excited. "You're going to scream for me, and you're going to love it. I know you will, baby."

"Oh God." She tossed her head on the pillow but couldn't help allowing her body to relax marginally.

She felt the device begin to penetrate the tight hole. At first, the piercing sensation was mild, but as the length and thickness increased, the steady, building fire began to shoot through her body.

She tensed, but Cole didn't ease up. She cried out as it grew brighter, then began begging as pain bloomed in her anus. But she wasn't begging him to stop.

"It hurts," she screamed out. "Oh God, Cole. Cole please—"

He didn't relent, instead, the fingers of his other hand moved to her pulsing sex. There, they stroked and petted her clit until she was thrusting, pushing into his hand, crying out as the movement pushed the plug deeper into her ass.

She could feel her muscles stretching, protesting but eventually giving way to the thick intruder invading it. She bucked against her ropes, rearing back, writhing under the lash of burning pain, and equally burning pleasure.

"Damn you!" Her voice was hoarse, enraged from the building kaleidoscope of sensations rushing through her body.

The fiery heat of the invasion, the slow steady buildup of pain, the resulting agonizing pleasure, so overwhelmed her senses that she felt dazed with it, awash in a darkly sensual reality where nothing existed except the slow, steady invasion of her ass, and the soft, too light caresses to her throbbing clit.

Long minutes later she jerked harshly as the last inch of the plug passed the tight anal ring, leaving seven inches of hard thick dildo lodged inside her. She squirmed, fighting to accustom herself to the sensation. Cole chose that moment to land his hand heavily on her ass again. Tess screamed, her muscles tightening around the plug, inflicting a disastrous form of ecstasy.

"Now, Tess," Cole growled. "Now, I get to eat that pretty pussy."

Chapter Eight

Tess's cries were echoing in his head, throbbing in his cock. Cole couldn't remember a time he had been so turned on, so hot and ready to fuck. He wanted to plunge his cock as deep, as hard up her tight cunt as he could. He wanted to slam it inside her, master her with the brutality of a fucking so lustful that she would find it impossible to leave the only man who could give it to her.

But he knew, the longer he could keep her hanging on the edge of the sensations ripping through her, the more she would crave it later. He was a slave to the need to be the one who pleasured her.

The piercing of her ass with that plug had been the most erotic, satisfying thing he had done in his life. He wondered if she was even aware of how loud she had begged for more, how many times she had pleaded with him to push it hard inside her, to take her. He doubted it. Submissives rarely remembered that first time, those first long minutes that the plug, or a hot, thick cock invaded their ass.

It was the pain and pleasure combined. The needs, so shocking, so consuming, that they dazed the mind to the point that the submissive rarely remembered begging for it.

"Fuck me," Tess still begged, her voice was thick and desperate as her cunt leaked the honeyed cream of her need.

And he would fuck her. Soon.

He lifted a small, oblong metal device from the tray. It was attached to a long cord with a control box at the end. A silver bullet, it was called. So tiny it appeared harmless, but the effects of its internal vibrations would send Tess into such a haze of rapture that she would never forget it.

He inserted the three-inch long device into her cunt. His cock clenched at the closed fist tightness he encountered as he pressed it past the fullness of the plug lodged in her ass and moved it to the back of her pussy. He positioned the little device for maximum vibration against her G-spot then withdrew. He set the control on low, a gentle, stroking vibration that nonetheless caused her to flinch. Then he set about feeding himself from her cunt.

He lapped at her pussy, just as he had once promised her he would. Gentle strokes into her vagina with his tongue that had her bucking against his mouth, begging for more. Her body was sheened with sweat, her breathing harsh, her cries desperate as he tongued her, stroked her. And she tasted so damned good he couldn't help himself but to thrust his tongue as deep inside her as he could go, and draw more of her into his mouth.

Cole was on fire for her. He knew his control was slipping, something that never happened, something he had never had to fight to keep before. But he had to prepare her, he couldn't allow himself to unwittingly hurt her. Tess was everything to him. His heart, his soul, the happiness he had always believed he would never find. She teetered between erotic pain and the pain that could irrevocably damage her sexuality forever. If he wasn't careful, extremely careful, then he would destroy both of them. Because Cole knew he couldn't go much longer without her.

So he tamped down his own lusts, stroked her gently, gauged her need and advanced the speed of the vibrator accordingly. She was bucking in his hands now, nearing that point of no return. Reluctantly, he moved back from her dripping vagina, licked back, circled her clit with his tongue. Then he turned, lying on his back, positioning himself to suck the swollen, engorged bud into his mouth as he edged the speed of the vibrator higher.

She exploded, her body tensed. Her scream was strangled, breathless, as her body bowed, jerked, then began a repeated shudder that signaled the beginning of her orgasm. He tightened his lips on her clit, flicked it with his tongue and held her hips with easy strength when the hot, volcanic rush of her release began to rush through her body.

Tess was dying. She knew she was dying and she eagerly embraced the exquisite rush of painful pleasure that threw her over the brink. Her body was jerking uncontrollably, her orgasm filling her body, pumping through her blood, spasming her uterus as it tore through her. She could feel the hard vibration inside her, Cole's lips at her clit, blending into a raging storm she knew she wouldn't survive. Hard shudders rushed over her; pleasure unlike anything she could have conceived tore her apart. And in a distant part of her mind, she wondered if she would ever be the same again. If she survived it.

She screamed against the torrent, but couldn't fight it. She could feel her fluids gushing through her pussy as it spasmed, and Cole's mouth moving to catch them with a hard, male groan. His tongue speared inside her tortured sex, triggering another hard shudder, another gush of fluids until finally, she collapsed mindlessly against her ropes, dazed, stripped of strength.

Small tremors still assaulted her. The never-ending pulse of her climax didn't go away easily. She could hear Cole, a hard, brutal male groan echoing through the room as his body jerked against her. Had he come? Had he been inside her and she didn't know it? It didn't matter. She was drifting on a haze of pleasure so weak, so astounding that she couldn't think, and didn't want to.

"Tess?" Cole's voice was tender, warm as he moved behind her. "Are you okay, baby?"

She felt the ropes loosening, his hands calloused and gentle on her skin as he untied her, helped her to stretch out on the bed. She lay boneless, so satiated she could barely move. She was aware of Cole moving along the bed beside her, turning her over to her back, his expression, when she looked up at him, was concerned, gentle.

"Sleepy," she whispered. And she was. So tired, so emotionally and physically drained she could barely stay awake.

"Sleep, Tess." He kissed her cheek gently. "Rest, baby. We start again tomorrow."

⚜ ⚜ ⚜

Cole lay down beside her, drawing the quilt over them, ignoring the pulse of his still throbbing cock. He had climaxed with Tess, but it wasn't enough. He needed to be buried inside her, feeling her, tight and hot, enclosing him with her satin heat.

And he knew the fight wasn't finished. Accepting the pain-filled pleasure would be the easy part for Tess. Submitting to him would be the hard part. Giving in to him, no matter what he asked of her, no matter what he demanded for her sexual pleasure, would be the fight. One he looked forward to. He knew Tess better than she knew herself. He knew, from her father telling him about the books her mother had found, what turned her on. It wasn't the pain, it was the domination, the submission into the sexual extremes that she craved. She wanted to fight. She wanted to be vanquished, and he wanted to give it to her.

He pulled her against him, luxuriating in the warmth of her body, her very presence. He had dreamed of this for two years. He knew the moment he met Tess that she held a part of him that no other woman ever could. The thought of it had tormented him, racked him with lust. In the past months, it had grown worse. He lived and breathed daily with the need for her. It was like a fever burning his loins that he couldn't escape.

And now he had her. By Valentine's night, her final lesson, when her final erotic dream was fulfilled, she would know who mastered her body and her heart.

Chapter Nine

Tess was sore. Her entire body throbbed, protesting her wakefulness. The muscles of her legs were stiff and burning, her arms and even her breasts were sore.

"Open your eyes, Tess. We have to remove the plug and you need a hot bath." Cole's voice was firm, brooking no refusal.

Her eyes snapped open, her head turning to him, her eyes focusing on the savage features of his face.

"You left that thing in me?" she bit out incredulously. He arched a single brow.

"Your ass was tight, Tess. It needs to accustom itself to stretching before you'll ever be able to take my cock there."

Her heart slammed into her ribs.

"Go to the bathroom, then come back here. If you try to remove it yourself, I'll tie you back down and leave you there the rest of the day."

He meant it. She saw his determination in the hard lines of his face. "Take it out first," she said instead.

He shook his head. "Do as I say, Tess. I have a reason for my demands, baby."

Tess frowned, but she knew she did not want to experience the torture of being tied down and frothing with need. And she knew he would make her froth. He would torture her, then leave her to suffer in her arousal. She wasn't ready to take that chance yet, not after last night.

So she rose from the bed, walking gingerly to the bathroom. After relieving her most pressing need, she brushed her teeth and washed her face, then returned to the bedroom. Her stomach rolled with nerves, as she wondered how Cole planned to continue the sensual torture he had started last night.

"On your knees." He nodded to the bed, standing beside it, naked and sporting an erection that resembled a weapon.

His cock was the largest she had ever seen, nearly as thick as her wrist, with a bulging, flared head that made her mouth water at the sight.

Tess went to the bed, assuming the position she knew he wanted. She trembled as his hand caressed the cheeks of her rear. His fingers ran down the crease of her ass until he gripped the plug, pulling it slowly, gently, free of her bottom.

"Stay still," he ordered her before she could move. "Under your cabinet are some personal supplies I bought for you. From now on you will use them whenever I tell you to do so. Understood?"

"Yes," she whispered, feeling her cunt burn, moisten as he ran his hands over her ass.

"I'm not going to fuck you now because to be honest, I don't think I can keep my cock out of your ass. But I need relief, baby."

He moved around the bed then, turning her as he faced her, his cock aiming at her mouth. Tess licked her lips. She opened them as the purpled head nudged against them. She heard his hard groan as she closed her lips around his cock, taking him, opening her throat to take that last inch possible.

One of his hands gripped his cock, to assure he didn't give her more than she could take, the other twisted in her hair. The sharp bite of pain had her mouth tightening around his cock, her throat working on the head as he cried out in pleasure. He wasn't willing to prolong his own pleasure this morning though. His thrust in and out of her mouth with deep, hard strokes, holding her still as he groaned repeatedly at the pleasure she was bringing him. Then, she felt his cock jerk, throb, and the pulse of his sperm filling her mouth as he cried out his release.

Cole was breathing hard when he pulled back from her, his cock was still engorged, still ready for her, but he did nothing more.

"Go bathe, Tess, before I do something neither of us is ready for. Come down to breakfast when you're finished."

Tess stood up, watching him fight for control. "Is Father home?" she asked.

He shook his head. "Not yet. He'll be back the night before the party. You're mine until then, Tess. Can you handle it?"

Her eyes narrowed at his tone of voice, the suggestion that she couldn't.

"I can handle you any day of the week." *Damn my mouth*, she groaned inwardly as the words poured from her lips.

His lips quirked. They both knew better.

"We'll see. Go bathe. I'll lay out what I want you to wear this morning. The servants have been given the rest of the week off as well, so there's just you and me for a while."

Tess bit her lip. She wasn't certain if that was a good thing or not.

"Go." He indicated the bathroom door. "Come downstairs when you're ready."

⚜ ⚜ ⚜

An hour later Tess walked down the spiraling stairs, barefoot and wearing more clothes than she thought he would lay out for her but decidedly less than she wanted to wear. The long, silk negligee made her feel sexy, feminine. It covered her breasts but was cut low enough that if he wanted them out, he would have no problems. There were no panties included, but the black silk shielded that fact. She would have been uncomfortable in something he could have seen right through.

His note had stated that he would await her in the kitchen, and there he was. Dressed in sweatpants and nothing else, his thick black hair still damp, looking sexier than any man had a right to look. And he was smiling at her. Even his eyes were filled with a lazy, comfortable expression as he set two plates of eggs, bacon and toast beside full coffee cups.

"You're right on time. breakfast is ready." He pulled out her chair, indicating that she should sit.

Tess took her seat gingerly. The soreness of her muscles was much better, but her thighs and rear were still tender.

"Sore?" He brushed a kiss over her bare shoulder, causing her to jerk in startled reaction.

She turned her head, looking up at him as he straightened and moved to his own chair.

"A little." She cleared her throat.

"It will get easier," he promised. "Now eat. We'll talk later, after you've been fed."

Breakfast, despite her initial misgivings, was filled with laughter. Cole was comfortable and his easy humor began to show. His dry wit kept her chuckling and the wicked sparkle in his eyes kept her body sizzling, kept her anticipating later, praying he would fuck her. The longer he waited, the hotter she got. She didn't know if she would survive it much longer.

Finally, after the dishes were finished, he drew her through the house into the comfortable living room. A fire crackled in the corner of the room where a large, thick pillow mattress had been laid.

"Sit down, we need to talk." He drew her down on the mattress, then onto her back as he lay beside her.

"Look, I don't much feel like talking," she finally said in frustration. "Let's just cut to the chase here,

Cole. There are things I evidently like, that you enjoy doing. I don't want to talk about them. Just do them."

She stared up at him, narrowing her eyes, warning him that she too had her limits. He propped his head on his hand, regarding her with a curious expression.

"I expected more of a fight," he said, a vague question in his voice.

Tess sighed, sitting up and staring into the fire as she ran the fingers of one hand through her hair.

"How extreme do you intend to get?" she finally asked, glancing at him as he reclined beside her.

He reached over, his fingers trailing down her hair. "How extreme do you want me to get, Tess?" he asked. "I can give you whatever you want, anything you want. But I have my own needs, and they will have to be satisfied as well."

"Such as?" she asked him, keeping her voice low, stilling the tremor that threatened to shake it.

"I like the toys, Tess. I like using them, and I'm dying to use them on you. I like spanking you. I like watching your pretty pussy and the rounded cheeks of your ass turning red. I like hearing you scream because you don't know if it hurts or if it's the pleasure killing you. I want to see your eyes filled with dazed pleasure as I push your limits." He laid it out for her pretty well, she thought with an edge of silent mockery, and still didn't answer a damned thing.

"How far will you go?" she asked.

"How far will you let me go?" he countered.

Tess had a feeling she would have few limits, but she wasn't willing to tell him that. "You evidently have plans. I'd like to know what they are."

Cole sighed. "Some things are better left up to the pleasure of the moment. Let's wait and see what happens."

Tess licked her lips nervously. Evidently her father had told him about the debacle with the books her mother had found. He wouldn't have known about them otherwise. She took a deep, hard breath.

"Does it concern other men?" she finally asked.

His eyes lit up with arousal. Tess lowered her head to her knees. God, she didn't know if she could.

"You want it, Tess." He moved behind her, sitting up to pull her against him as he whispered the words in her ear. "You've wanted it for a long time, baby, everything I've planned. Just settle down, and we'll take it step by step."

Tess was fighting to control her breathing, her heart rate. She was terrified of him, and of herself.

"I can't, if Father found out—"

"Tess, your father knows," he said gently. "Why do you think your mother divorced him? She didn't want sex, let alone what he needed. Your father knew when those books were found what you needed. Just as he knows what I need."

Embarrassment coursed through her body. She remembered coming home from college, her mother raging at her, the humiliation of the accusations she had thrown at Tess. It was one of the few times her father had put his foot down. Then he had pulled her into his study and uncomfortably informed her that sexuality was a personal thing, and none of his or her mother's business.

"Your sister—?" She left the question hanging.

"Knows what he wants and enjoys it. That's the key point, Tess. You have to enjoy it, otherwise, it brings me no pleasure. Your pleasure is most important. What you want, what you need."

His hands were at her abdomen, softly stroking the nervous muscles there. His lips brushed over her shoulder, her neck.

"I don't want a toy, Tess," he promised her. "Or a woman who doesn't know her mind and speak up accordingly. But in the bedroom, that is where I want the woman I know you are. If you want to fight me, then fight. If you want to submit, then do so. If you want to be tied down and dominated, let me know. All of it, I can give you and enjoy. But if you ever reach a limit, you have to tell me. If I ever suggest something you don't want or can't handle, then you have to speak up. And after that, unless you ask for it, it will never be approached again. So be very careful in the pleasures you deny yourself."

She lifted her head from her knees.

"And when you're tired of me?" she asked him.

"What if you grow tired of me first?" he asked her then. "It goes both ways, Tess. If we can't give the other what they need, then there's no point in going on. Do you agree?"

Her hands clenched at her knees. "I agree," she whispered.

"There are no rules, Tess. But from this point on, no means no. If you don't want it, then you say the word. Understand?"

She nodded nervously.

"Each night, I'll push you further. Each night, you'll learn something new about yourself." His hands moved to her arms, caressing the tight muscles, easing the nervousness locking them up. "Don't be frightened of me, Tess. Or of yourself."

"No other women." She wanted it clear from the beginning. "I don't know if I can even handle another man. But you can have no other women."

"I don't want another woman, Tess," he assured her. "And there will be no other men, unless it's something I decide." His voice hardened. "There is a particular pleasure in sharing your woman that you may never understand. But not just any man would be worthy of the privilege, baby, trust me."

"If you don't fuck me now, I'll walk out of this house and I won't come back," she finally breathed roughly. "I'm tired of waiting, Cole."

She had turned the tables on him then, she moved before he could stop her, turning and pressing against his shoulders until he laid back on the mattress. He was already hard, and she was already wet. His cock tented the front of his pants, hiding him from her. Hooking her hands in the waistband she pulled them down, lifting them over the thick erection and jerking them from his legs.

"I wondered when you would get tired of waiting," he said with a smile, though his gaze was hot, wickedly lustful.

Tess jerked the gown over her head, then moved up his body. She heard his hard breath when her damp folds grazed his cock, but she continued on. She wanted his kiss. She was dying for it.

As her lips touched his, his arms went around her, turning her, flipping her onto her back as he rose above her. His tongue pierced her mouth, his lips slanting over hers as he turned the caress into a carnal feast. Tess moaned brokenly, feeling the tenderness, the utter warmth of his touch, his body above hers, the easy strength of his muscles as he kept her close against him.

"My dick is so hard I won't last five minutes inside you," he bit out. "Are you on the pill, or do I need a condom?"

"Pill," she gasped. She didn't want anything between them. She wanted to feel him when he came, feel his seed spurting hard inside her. She protected herself, and not just during a relationship. She maintained that protection.

"Damn, Tess, I'm almost scared to fuck you, you're so damned tight," he growled as his hand smoothed over her pussy, his finger testing her vagina.

Tess arched into the penetration, her hungry moan shocking her as her body begged for more.

His lips trailed along her neck, moving steadily down, down to the hard, sensitive tips of her breasts.

When his mouth covered one, her womb contracted. Oh yeah. That was good. SO good. His tongue rasped over the tip, his mouth suckling at her with a strong motion that left her quivering. Then he nibbled at the small bud, the slight pinch driving her arousal higher with the edge of pain.

"You're so hot you're burning me alive," he growled, moving back to her lips, searing them with his kiss.

"Burn more then," she panted. "Please, Cole. Take me now."

He rose above her, moving between her thighs, spreading them wide, as she watched his cock pulse.

"It might hurt," he warned her, breathing heavy. "Damn, Tess, I've never had a pussy so tight it burned my finger before."

She rolled her hips, tormented by the tip of his cock as it nudged against her vagina. "That's okay," she whimpered. "You can handle it."

He surged inside her.

The breath left Tess's body as it bowed, a strangled scream tearing from her throat at the forced separation of her sensitive vaginal muscles. The burning pleasure/pain consumed her, traveling through her as she twisted against the thick cock lodged inside her.

"Sweet mercy, Tess," Cole cried out as he came over her heavily, his elbows bracing to take his weight. His hips rolled in a smooth motion between her thighs that sent sharp darts of ecstasy traveling through her body.

❋ ❋ ❋

He wasn't going to last long. Cole knew he didn't have a prayer of it. The best he could hope for was that Tess wouldn't either. He grabbed her hips, his face buried in the damp curve of her neck as he began a strong, steady motion inside her body.

Her cunt was so tight it burned, so slick and sweet he could stay inside her forever, if only he could hold his release back that long. There wasn't a chance. She twisted against him, her hips lifting for him, her legs wrapping around his waist as she took him deeper, screaming out with the sensations his hard thrusts sent through her.

Cole groaned at her heat. He pushed into her harder, his thrusts gaining in speed, spearing inside her, sliding through sensitive tissue that gripped him, fought to hold him. Her body tightened further until finally, her pussy began to quake around him as she cried out, jerking in his arms, her orgasm slamming into her at the same time he lost control.

Cole heard his howl of ecstasy, her strangled scream of release as he began coming inside her. Heat enveloped him, seared him, filled his body and soul as her hold on him tightened.

"Tess. God, Tess, baby—" He didn't think the hard flares of pleasure would ever end. Prayed they never did. They shot up his spine, through his dick, and dissolved the hard, lonely core to his heart. This woman was his. And before the week was over, he'd prove it to her.

Chapter Ten

For Tess, the days continued in a haze of pleasure. Cole was alternately gentle and masterful, seductive and surprising. He pushed her as he warned he would. He tied her down and tormented her with his skillful tongue and a variety of sexual toys meant to both tease and torment. Throughout the day she wore the silky gowns he laid out for her, and roamed the house with him. They talked and laughed, made love and lust in a variety of rooms and positions. But more importantly, Tess learned about the man.

The privileged, driven man whose incredible intelligence often hid a man of intense emotions. She would catch glimpses of it during certain conversations or after a session of intense, almost brutal lovemaking. His expression would be concerned, loving, as though despite his needs, his desires, he feared hurting her.

He still made her wear the butt plug for several hours daily. Before it was time to remove it, he would fuck her slow and easy, his cock sliding forcefully inside the ultra-tight passage of her vagina. The sensation was incredible. Tess would scream for him, beg, plead for mercy as the streaking pain and pleasure assaulted her body. Her climaxes tore her apart with the sensations, leaving her heaving against him, her juices exploding around his cock and triggering his own climax.

Their time was slowly coming to a close, though. On the sixth day, Tess dressed in yet another gown. The new one was a Grecian design that fell to her feet, with small golden silken ropes crossing over the front from her abdomen to beneath her breasts. She was barefoot again, but she knew that Cole would be as well. He wore clothes easy to remove. She grinned. For the most part, they went naked through the house anyway.

They ate breakfast quickly. Tess knew Cole had something planned for the day, but she wasn't certain what. She learned quickly a bit later, though. As she lay on the mattress in front of the fire Cole pulled four massively heavy weights from the corner of the room. He placed one at each corner of the mattress, then gave her that dark, commanding look that set her blood on fire.

"Last lesson," he whispered, tying a length of silken rope on the metal rings welded to them.

"Take off your gown and lie on your stomach."

A tremor of arousal shook her body as she pulled the gown from her body. Cole then buckled a leather band at each ankle and wrist before attaching the ropes to them. It left her spread, defenseless, with just enough play in the rope for him to place large, wide pillows beneath her body, levering her several inches above the mattress. Under her hips he placed yet another, leaving her ass defenseless, open to his gaze.

"Who owns your body?" he whispered, running his finger along the flaming crease of her cunt as his other hand stroked her buttocks.

"I do." Her voice was rough. She was in the right position for punishment; she didn't want to waste it.

His hand landed on her ass with stinging force. She flinched, cried out at the flare of heat in her flesh and deep within her cunt.

"Who owns your body, Tess?" he asked her again.

"Not you," she cried out. She needed more, again. She wanted him to set her ass to burning, because she knew what it would do to the rest of her body. Her breasts were swollen, her nipples hard and hurting.

He slapped her again. "Who owns your body?"

"Me." The haze of arousal was dulling reality now. His hand landed again.

"Need any help, Cole?" For a moment, Tess thought she imagined the smooth, cultured voice coming from the doorway.

She opened her eyes, her head turning, her eyes widening in mortification at the sight of the man leaning casually against the doorframe.

Jesse Wyman was one of the vice presidents at her father's company, answerable only to Cole and her father. He was as darkly handsome as Cole was, but more refined, not as large or savage looking. His green eyes were dark now, filled with lust rather than calculation, and the bulge in his pants looked more than impressive.

"Cole?" Was this part of his plan? If not, her suddenly dripping pussy may just get her into trouble.

"Say no and he walks away." Cole's voice was hot, suggestive. "Do you remember the book your mother threw the biggest fit over, Tess?" he whispered hotly. "The woman was tied down, her ass raised, her pussy, her mouth, and her ass at the mercy of the hero and his best friend? Meet my best friend, baby."

Tess quivered. She could feel Cole's hand stroking over her heated bottom, Jesse's eyes following the caress. Her heart labored heavily in excitement, the blood thundering through her veins. She had always wondered what it would feel like. Wondered if she could handle two men at once.

"Cole—?" She was frightened, too. The unfamiliar longings were shuttling through her body, making her shake in indecision.

"Tess," he whispered. "It won't be the last time I ask it of you. I promise you, baby, you'll love it."

She could hear the excitement in his voice, the arousal as Jesse started into the room, his hands going to the buttons of his white dress shirt.

"God, you two do this all the time?" she gasped.

"Just sometimes. Just when it's important, Tess. When we know it's needed. And baby, you need it." His finger dipped into her pussy, pushing through the frothing juice that dripped from it.

Tess groaned, pushing back into his finger as Jesse dropped his shirt to the floor. His chest was muscular and deeply tanned. His green eyes glittered with rising lust. Tess watched, mesmerized as his hand went to the fastening of his slacks.

"She's beautiful," Jesse growled as he kicked his shoes off then disposed of his slacks and boxers. "Has she been a good girl for you, Cole?" His voice was suggestive, searing her with the implication that she needed to be punished.

His hands tested the restraints at her wrists, then his fingers feathered over her cheek. Tess shuddered at the caress.

"Tess usually finds a way to be naughty, don't you, baby?" Cole's hand landed on her bottom in a light smack.

She jerked, whimpering. Dear God, they were both going to punish her, pleasure her? She felt faint from excitement, her body tingling. She nearly climaxed when Jesse came to his knees beside her, his erection not as large as Cole's, but nearly. It was thick, pulsing, the head throbbing. His hand touched her hair, his eyes locked with hers, and then Tess understood why Cole had propped pillows beneath her whole body. To raise her high enough to keep her arms stretched wide, and still in position for any cock sucking required. Her mouth watered at the thought, then opened in a cry of surprise when Cole's hand struck her ass again.

"Naughty Tess." His voice was filled with amusement.

"Beautiful Tess," Jesse's voice was a low growl of pleasure. "Her butt pinkens so well. Does it stretch as easily?"

"My ass," Cole grunted. "I haven't fucked it yet, so you can't either."

Jesse grunted but said nothing more. A second later, Tess felt his lips at her shoulder, his teeth scraping over her skin as his hands reached beneath her on either side to cup her full, swollen breasts. His fingers gripped her nipples, pinching lightly as she groaned at the hot little flare of pain. She jerked at the caress, fighting to breathe as she felt Cole's hand descend on her ass once again. She was bucking at each blow, crying out as Jesse alternately soothed and inflamed her nipples, his mouth on her neck, nibbling, licking at her, keeping her poised on a pinnacle of arousal so sharp it was agony.

It was then that Tess felt Cole move away from her for a second. When he returned, his finger, thickly lubricated, began to work its way up her still tight anus. He slid the finger in easily, though her muscles pinched at the entrance. He pulled back slowly, then two broad fingers were working up the tight channel, spreading her, thrusting lightly inside as she cried out, begging for more.

Jesse's fingers tightened on her nipples, then caressed them, tightened again, caressed again. Cole's fingers, three now, worked slowly up her small back entrance, his voice hot and encouraging as she opened to him, her muscles stretching as it sent fire flaring through her body.

"I'm going to fuck your ass today, Tess," he growled. "I'm going to lubricate you real good, baby, then I'm going to work my cock up your tight ass and listen to you scream for me. Will you scream for me, baby?"

Scream? She couldn't breathe. She was gasping for breath as Jesse pulled the pillows from beneath her body, lying down beside her, his strong arms holding her up as he pushed his head under her to catch a hard, turgid nipple in his mouth.

There was enough slack to the ropes holding her wrists now that she could partially prop herself up with her hands. Jesse helped her hold her weight, splayed as she was, with his hard hands beneath her breasts. But the strong suction, strong nips and rasping tongue on her tender nipples were driving her crazy.

Her head tossed as she panted for breath. Cole's fingers were working further up her ass now, spilling fire and hot, dark rapture as he slowly stretched her, his fingers spreading inside her to part the heated passage.

"Jesse is going to fuck your tight pussy for me, Tess," Cole promised her, his voice rough from his lust. "After I work my cock up your sweet ass, he's going to take that tight cunt. You'll be stretched and full baby, both of us working you, fucking you."

His explicit words caused her womb to spasm painfully, her body to bow involuntarily as she pushed against his fingers.

"Oh yes, baby, you want it, don't you?" Pleasure filled his voice. "You want to be taken, filled and fucked like the sweet treasure you are."

His voice was awed, enraptured, as though it were she giving him a gift, rather than the other way around. As Cole spoke, Jesse pushed his body beneath hers, sliding easily in the space the cushions had once taken until she was draped over him, his cock nestling at the soaked lips of her bare cunt.

"Tess, I wish you could see how beautiful you look," Cole groaned as he moved back until Jesse could get into position. "Your sweet cunt dripping all over his cock, soaking it. Your ass raised and ready for me. Are you ready for me, baby?"

Tess whimpered. Was she ready? The thought of his cock, so thick and hard pushing up her ass, was at once terrifying and exhilarating.

"I think you're ready." She felt him move into position as Jesse reached around, pulling the cheeks of her ass apart.

"Relax for me, Tess," Cole groaned. "I promise, it's gonna be so good."

She felt the head of his cock begin its entrance inside her. Slowly, easing inside her, stretching her until she was screaming out at the shocking pain of the entrance. Pain and pleasure, it seared her, held her immobile as he worked his cock inside her, inch by inch.

Jesse held her flesh apart, but his lips caressed her face, whispering encouragement, dark, naughty words that made her need for the sexual pain flare higher, hotter. His voice was approving, tender.

"It's okay, Tess," he soothed her as she bucked, her eyes tearing from the pain, though she didn't want it to stop. She never wanted it to stop. "Don't fight it, Tess," he urged. "Cole's cock is thick, but not too thick. You can take it." He pulled her flesh apart further, easing the shocking pain as Cole continued to tunnel inside her.

"Tess, are you okay, baby?" She could hear the strain in his voice, the hot vibrating vein of lust and possession, caring and tenderness.

"Please—" she gasped as he halted the slow, gliding entrance.

The head of his cock had just passed the tight ring of muscles, the flared tip stretching it wide as she fought to accustom herself to his large cock filling her there.

"More, baby?" he asked her, his hand smoothing down her back.

"More," she cried, her hips easing back on the burning lance. "More. Please, Cole. More."

He began to ease further inside her as the tip of Jesse's cock throbbed at the entrance to her pussy. A slow, steady stroke had Cole filling her ass completely, his hard groan as he sank into her up to his balls echoed in the room.

Tess was crying out repeatedly now, her muscles clenching on him, her body accepting the pain as a torturous pleasure she couldn't deny any longer. Her hips moved against him, driving him deeper, lodging the pulsing head of Jesse's cock just inside her vaginal entrance as Cole pulled back, then pushed forward again.

"Yes," she screamed out as he began an easy thrusting motion inside her ass. "Oh God, Cole. Fuck me. Please fuck me!"

He pushed harder inside her. Once. Twice. Then stilled. Tess would have protested, but she lost her breath. Beneath her, Jesse began to push his hard cock into the tiny, tiny entrance of her vagina. Cole's cock filled her ass to bursting, leaving little room in her snug pussy. But Jesse didn't let that hinder him. Groaning, praising the ultra-tight fit, he sank slowly into the heated depths until he was lodged in to the hilt.

Reality ceased to exist. She didn't even know when Jesse had reached up to release the leather manacles or when Cole had released those at her ankles. But she was on her hands and knees, sandwiched between them, begging for more. Pleading for the hard thrusts of their cocks inside her as they set up a slow, rhythmic thrusting motion that threatened to drown her in pleasure. She was insane with the burning ecstasy spearing her body. She moved against them, taking them, urging them on until their building thrusts were powerful strokes inside her. They were fucking her hard and fast now, each man groaning, praising her, crying out as she tightened on them.

"Cole," she screamed out his name as she felt her orgasm building. "Oh God, Cole, I can't stand it."

"You can, Tess," he groaned, levering over her body as his hips powered inside her. "You can, baby. Take it. Take it, Tess. Cum for me, baby. Cum for me now." He surged inside her as she tightened around him.

Beneath her, Jesse had clasped her waist hard, his hips slamming into hers, and despite their speed, both men kept in perfect synchronization with the hard thrusts of their cocks inside her body.

Tess couldn't stop her screams, couldn't stop the sensations that tightened her body. The boiling pressure, the hard, piercing pleasure/pain was too much for her untutored body to take for long. When she climaxed, she wailed out at the explosion, tightening on them further, her ass and her cunt milking the cocks possessing her until she heard their shattered male groans and felt the hard, spurting jets of their sperm filling each hole.

Her orgasm shuddered through her body, over and over. Her muscles clenched on their cocks as they exploded inside her, making them cry out around her, jerk against her as her cunt and her ass drew on their flesh, shuddered around it, burned them with her release until she fell against Jesse gasping, boneless.

"Son of a bitch, Cole," Jesse's voice was harsh, weary now. "She's drained me."

Cole pulled free of her and collapsed on the mattress, helping Jesse to lower Tess between them. Once there, he pulled her against his body, his hands running over her back, his lips caressing her temple as she fought to regain her breath.

"You're mine, Tess," he whispered, stopping her heart with the emotion she heard in his voice. "Taken by me. Held by me. I won't let you escape me again."

She would have answered him, but shock held her immobile when she heard the enraged scream of her mother from the doorway.

"You dirty whore! Just like your father. You're just like your father—!"

Chapter Eleven

"Oh my God!" Humiliation sped through Tess's system seconds later as Cole and Jesse jumped to hide her from sight.

They jerked their pants from the floor, shielding Tess as they dressed quickly. Cole's body was tight with fury as Tess fumbled with her gown, her fingers shaking so badly she could barely get it over her head.

Turning to her, still shielding her, Cole helped her untangle the material and ease it over her head.

"I'm sorry, baby," he whispered, his lips feathering over her hair as he straightened the gown.

Tess shook her head, feeling the heat that traveled over her face. With a final touch of his fingertips to her cheek, he turned to her mother.

"How the hell did you get in?" His voice was furious as he faced Ella Delacourte, dark and warning.

"I didn't come here to talk to you, perverted bastard that you are. Look how you corrupted my daughter. You're just like that trashy, home-wrecking sister of yours." Ella was screeching now.

Tess felt her face flame in shame as she stood to her feet, her legs shaking from her exertions and her fear. Dear God, how had her mother gotten into the house?

"Mother, why are you here?" Tess's voice was thick with tears and confusion.

She wasn't ashamed that she had experienced the sexuality of the act. But being caught in it was mortifying. And by her mother!

"I came to see why you were here after I found out your father and his tramp were away for the week," she sneered. "You haven't even called me. I was worried."

The classic guilt trip from her mother any time Tess spent time with her father.

"Ella, control your tongue." Jesse's voice was hard and laced with warning. Tess looked at him in surprise. She had no idea Jesse knew her mother.

Ella cast the other man a look that should have withered him with shame. Jesse stood before her, his shoulders squared, his dark face furious.

"Tess, go shower or something." Cole drew her into his arms, kissing her head softly, his hands soothing on her back. "Let me take care of this."

Tess shook her head.

"I haven't needed you to fight my battles before this, Cole. I don't need you to do it now," she said. "I haven't done anything wrong—"

"Wrong?" Ella's voice was piercing. "You think fucking your perverted lover and his friend isn't wrong, Tess? I raised you better than to whore for some depraved bastard."

Tess trembled at the fury in her mother's voice.

"Ella!" Jesse's voice was a lash of cold, hard fury now. "Get the hell out of here before I escort you out. And I don't think you want me to have to do that."

The heated edge of fury in Jesse's voice surprised Tess. "Get her the hell out of here," Cole muttered to his friend.

"Would all of you just stop this?" Tess ran her fingers through her hair, hating the tremble in her hands as she faced her mother.

Years of being made to feel ashamed of her sexuality, of her needs as a woman, washed over her. She remembered the lectures from the time she was a child, on the depravities of sex and the sins of the flesh.

"Mother, I told you I'd be back after the party," she sighed, leaning against Cole for support, thankful in a way that she didn't have to hide from her mother now.

"How could you do this, Tess?" Ella's expression was livid, her gray eyes glittering with fury. "How could you have become so depraved?"

"Depraved?" Tess shook her head, sighing. "I'm just different from you. I'm sorry."

A tear escaped her eyes. She hated having her mother angry with her, just as she had hated leaving her father so long ago.

As she finished speaking, a movement behind her mother caught Tess's attention. Her father, tall and strong, his face coldly furious, moved into the room.

"Well, I guess you're satisfied," Ella sneered when she saw him. "She's just like you and that whore you married."

Missy was with her father, and for once, Tess saw anger lining the beautiful blonde's face.

"You're in my home, Ella," Missy reminded her, her slender body tense and lined with anger. "I suggest you leave it and consider what you're losing in this display you seem intent on. Tess isn't a child. She's a woman. Her lifestyle is none of your concern."

Fury pulsed through the room, nearly choking Tess.

"I can't believe you did this. That a child of mine would lower herself to the same games her father plays." Tess flinched under the cold, unrelenting judgment her mother was meting out.

"Ella!" Missy's voice was a lash of hot fury. "I will have you escorted from my home if you cannot speak to your daughter decently. What she does is no business of yours. She's a grown woman."

"And I don't need anyone fighting my battles for me," Tess bit out, more than surprised at the confident edge of power in her stepmother's voice. Missy with a backbone? She wouldn't have believed it.

"Do you know what she was doing here, Jason?" Ella screamed out at her ex-husband. "This has gone even further than the games you practice—"

"For God's sake, Ella!" Jason cursed furiously. "Listen to you. Do you think our daughter wants to hear this? Our problems don't involve her." Her father's face was ruddy with his own embarrassment. "I don't care what she was doing. I trust Cole to protect her, that's all I need to know."

"Well had you shown up a moment sooner—"

"Then I would have warned them of my arrival before entering the house," he growled in disgust as he cast Tess an apologetic look. "For pity's sake, stop humiliating Tess because of your own bitterness. This has gone too far."

Ella turned to Tess, her eyes hard, resentful. "Leave your belongings, Tess. You're going home with me. Now!"

When had she ever given her mother permission to order her around in such a manner? Tess watched her in growing confusion and pain. She had never known how angry, how bitter, her mother had become. And for what reason? She had often stated how her life was more secure without a man interfering in it.

"I won't leave, Mother." She felt Cole's hands tighten at her shoulders, the way his body tensed expectantly behind her.

Shock filled her mother's expression. "What did you say?" she gasped. "I won't leave—"

"You heard me…"

"He's using you, Tess," Ella said furiously. "You'll be nothing but his whore. He proved that today."

Tess shook her head. "I love him, Mother. I have for years and I was too scared to admit to it. But I'm even more frightened of being alone and bitter, without at least having this time with him."

Silence held the room. She thought she heard Cole whisper a reverent "Thank God." But she wasn't certain.

"You will," Ella screamed furiously, her fists clenching at her side, her eyes glittering wildly. "You won't stay with these monsters."

"Perhaps it's where I belong." Tess wanted to cry out at the hurt that flashed in her mother's eyes. "I love Cole, Mother, and I'm not ashamed of that, or what I've done. I enjoyed it."

Ella opened her mouth to say more.

"Don't speak, Ella," Jason snapped. "Keep your mouth shut and leave her the hell alone."

"You don't control me, Jason," Ella bit out, her body trembling. "You didn't while we were married and you don't now."

"Probably what her problem is," Cole whispered at Tess's ear.

Her eyes widened for a moment before she put her elbow in his hard stomach. He only chuckled.

"I will if you don't keep that viperous tongue quiet," he growled. "And trust me, Ella, you better be careful. You may find out the monsters you hate so much are more a part of you than you know."

"I'm not part of this." Jesse finally sighed as he finished dressing. "I'm heading out of here, boys and girls. See you at the office, Cole."

He slapped Cole on the shoulder before leaving the room. Ella's eyes followed him, narrowed, furious.

"Mother, perhaps you should leave as well." Tess took a hard, deep breath. "We'll discuss this later, when we're both calmer."

Ella turned back to her. The perfectly groomed cap of auburn hair framed a surprisingly young face. At forty-two, Ella Delacourte looked nearly a decade younger. But she was more bitter and vengeful than any woman twice her age, with a much harder life. "Come with me now, Tess, or I won't allow you back in my home." Ella's lips thinned as she stared at her daughter, ice coating her voice. "You'll no longer be a daughter of mine."

Tess trembled. She had never seen her mother so angry. "I'm sorry, Mother." She shook her head. "I can't."

Ella drew herself erect. She cast her ex-husband a dark look then turned and stalked from the house. Tess flinched as the front door slammed closed behind her.

"She'll settle down, Tess," Jason said gently. "You know how your mother gets." Tess ran her fingers through her hair as she took a hard, deep breath.

"She won't forgive me, Father," she said, her voice low, thick with tears. "Not ever. No more than she ever forgave you."

"Tess," Cole's voice was soft, gentle as his arms wrapped around her, holding her.

What a perfect feeling, she thought, to be held so tight, so warm against him. But how long would it last? How long could it last? She loved him, but how could he love her? Had her own desires, her unnatural needs lost her the love of the only man she had ever truly wanted?

Chapter Twelve

The question followed Tess through the rest of that night. Cole didn't come to her bed. For the first time in six nights, he wasn't beside her, tempting her, teasing her with his body, his lust. She lay in the middle of the big bed, staring silently up at the vaulted ceiling, the loneliness of the room smothering her. God help her, if she couldn't get through one night without him, how would she handle the rest of her life?

What had she done? Had her desire to experience with him everything his other women had been her downfall? Had her envy, her depravity, ruined the only chance she had to make him love her? She swallowed the tight knot of fear in her throat. Realistically, she had known that her chances of capturing his heart were slim. She just hadn't expected it to be over so soon.

Realizing she wouldn't be sleeping any time soon, Tess got up, pulling on the bronze silk robe that lay at the bottom of the bed and belting it firmly. She slipped her feet into soft, matching slippers and left the room. She would prefer to sit in the kitchen, drowning her sorrows in the chocolate mint ice cream her father kept on hand, rather than wallowing in them.

As she stepped into the hallway, she followed the bright light spilling from the kitchen further up the hall. She halted in surprise at the doorway. Dressed in a thick robe, her blonde hair attractively mussed, her surprisingly pretty face free of makeup, sat Missy, digging into a bowl of the ice cream, the box sitting temptingly in front of her.

"Great minds think alike?" Missy flashed her a smile as she looked up, waving the spoon in her hand at the cabinet. "Grab a bowl."

Tess walked to the cabinet and did just that, then sat down at the other side of the rounded table and began to spoon in a large portion.

"Nothing settles the nerves like Chocolate Mint," Missy sighed.

"I'm sorry," Tess apologized, genuinely regretful that she had caused her stepmother any pain. "I didn't expect Mother to show up."

Missy paused, her spoon suspended above her bowl as she flashed Tess a frown.

"Tess, I'm not upset for me," she said sincerely. "I'm upset for you and Cole. Your private choices should not be aired in such a manner. Cole was furious, of course, that she hurt you. But I was angry for your sake."

"Why?" Tess frowned. "We've never been close. We barely get along."

A knowing smile tipped Missy's pale lips.

"Tess, you fight with someone when you feel threatened, and when you care without a safety net, an assurance that you are cared for as well. I know that. I used to be the same way, until I met Jace."

Tess hunched her shoulders. Missy's assessment was much too close to the truth.

"That's how I knew you loved Cole." Missy dropped her next bombshell. "At first, it was just general sniping, but as he teased and flirted and pushed you, it became outright fighting on your side. I knew then your heart was involved."

Tess nearly choked on the spoonful of ice cream she was attempting to swallow. How could anyone, especially airhead Missy, who wasn't such an airhead after all, know her better than she knew herself?

"Have I lost him?" Tess couldn't keep the longing, the fear from her voice as she stared back at the other woman.

"Lost Cole?" Missy laughed in surprising amusement. "Tess, Cole has been fighting for your attention for over two years now. What the future will bring, I don't know. But I sincerely doubt you have anything to worry about for the present."

This did little ease to her worry.

"He hasn't returned." She shrugged, dropping her eyes to her bowl. "Maybe I disgusted him. Maybe I was supposed to refuse when Jesse came in?"

When Missy didn't answer, Tess risked a quick look. The other woman watched her sympathetically, warmly.

"Cole is different from other men," she said as Tess watched her worriedly. "How different, is up to you to discover. But I've known him all his life, and I know Cole doesn't play games. If he invited Jesse, then he wanted it, too. He wouldn't try to trap you, Tess, or hurt you. You have to trust him that far."

"I'm scared," Tess admitted, her eyes going back to the melting ice cream. "I don't know how to handle what I feel and what I want."

"Do any of us?" Missy's chuckle was self-mocking. "It takes meeting the man who can give us what we need, who knows, because it's what they need. I know, Tess, because that's what your father and I have. A relationship that fulfills what both of us need."

"Mother never loved him." Tess knew that, had known it for a long time.

"Your mother has to love herself first." Missy shrugged. "Now finish your ice cream. I'm sure Cole will be back before the party tomorrow, and he'll show you then how much he's missed you. I know he didn't want to leave and he hated going before talking to you first, but in this case, he assured me it was necessary."

What, Tess wondered, could have been so important that he couldn't even see her before leaving?

⚜ ⚜ ⚜

Tess waited, and she waited. All through the next day, while she was dressing for the party, and halfway through the boisterous, noisy affair she waited, and held onto the hope that he would be back that night. She gave up at nine. She set aside her glass of champagne, put away her hope and walked regally from the noisy ballroom and up the narrow steps that led to the Turret Room. She would pack and leave in the morning. She wasn't certain where she would go, but she was certain she couldn't risk staying here, or beg him to forgive her for something she didn't know if she would change.

The sexual dominance of the act had thrilled her. The utter thick, hot pleasure in Cole's voice had only spurred her on. She didn't know if it was something she would ever want again, but she knew experiencing it would be a memory she would always hold onto.

She kept her head down as she entered the room, going straight for the suitcase stored in the large walk-in closet just inside the room. She placed it on the luggage rack, opened it and re-entered the closet to collect the few things she had brought with her.

As she folded the articles of clothing, the tears began to fall. They were hot, blistering with pain, and shook her body as she tried to console herself that at least she had tried. For one time in her life, a very brief time, she was free.

She wiped at the tears, her breath hitching as she moved to the stone dresser to collect the clothing there, then she went to her bed and picked up her robe. The last article Cole had given her. It was then she saw the small, black velvet jeweler's box. She stopped, clutching the silk robe to her chest.

It was a ring. The diamond glittered with shards of blue and orange, intensifying the gold of the thick, simple band. Her hands shook, her body trembled. Her head raised, her eyes going to the shadows of the opened bathroom door.

"Shame on you, Tess," Cole chided her gently as he walked from the room where he waited. "To think I wouldn't come back. I'll have to punish you for that."

His chest was bare, his jeans rode low on his hips and fit tightly over the bulge beneath the material.

Tess took a deep, hard breath.

"You didn't call," she whispered as she saw the mask of cool determination on his face, the sparkle of warmth in his eyes that was so at odds with his expression. "You didn't say goodbye."

"If I had seen you, I wouldn't have left. And I had to leave or miss the jeweler before he left. You should have known I had a reason."

Cole's voice was cool, disapproving. His eyes were patient, wicked and warm. God, she could feel her cunt heating to lava temperature.

"You knew I would worry," she snapped out, ignoring the hope, the happiness surging inside her.

"Worry, but not have so little faith in me." There was an edge of hurt in his voice now, as though her tears, and the cause for them, pricked at his emotions. "After taking you, did you think I would let you go easily?"

A sob broke in her chest, another tear fell.

"I enjoyed it," she whispered brokenly. "You shouldn't love me."

"Tess," he whispered her name gently. "Don't you think I want it, too? That I didn't enjoy your pleasure as well? It was the first time, baby, and it won't be the last time. I love hearing your cries, feeling your pleasure, knowing you're dominated, submitting to me, no matter what I want. Tess, I love you more for it, not less."

"How?" she whispered brokenly, shaking her head. "How could you?"

"Do you want Jesse alone, Tess?" he asked her carefully. "Would you let him touch you, hold you, if I didn't ask you to do so?"

"No!" she burst out, realizing the idea was abhorrent to her. What she had done with Cole could never have been done without him.

He came closer to her, standing within inches of her, staring down at her with heated arousal, and something more. Something she was terrified to admit to seeing. What if she was wrong? What if it wasn't love she saw in his eyes?

Rather than taking her in his arms, he indicated to her to sit on the bed. Tess did so slowly as he reached around her and retrieved the box on the bed. As her eyes rounded in shock, he went to one knee before her, holding the box in front of her as he stared up at her in adoration.

"You're mine." He wasn't asking her anything. "Taken by me, Tess. Mine to hold and mine to love now."

He took the ring from the box, picked up her hand and slid the diamond firmly over her finger.

"Is this a proposal?" she asked huskily, incredulously.

"Hell no. I'm not asking you anything," he grunted. "With that smart-assed mouth of yours, you'd have me tying you down rather than loving you the way I want to."

"Loving me?" she whispered as he pushed her down on the bed, following her with his heated, hard body.

"Loving you, Tess," he promised. "With everything I have. With all I am, I love you."

His lips covered hers, his tongue pushing past her lips with a determination, a heat she couldn't deny. Her hands grasped his shoulders, her body arching to him as she groaned into the kiss. His lips ate at hers, his tongue plundering her mouth wickedly as his hands worked behind her back at the zipper of her dress, then stripped it quickly from her body.

He never broke the kiss, or lost the heat of his arousal as he stripped his pants from his hips, kicking them from his muscular legs. He didn't miss a beat as he ripped the silk of her panties from her body.

"Mine," he growled as his head finally raised, only to rake his lips down her neck in a fiery caress, his tongue licking at her skin, his hands lifting her against him as his lips arrowed to her breast. There, they covered a hard, engorged nipple, sucking it into his mouth with a groan of arousal.

Tess arched to him, crying out brokenly at the fierce thrust of pleasure that clenched her womb and her vagina at the same time. Like a punch of heated ecstasy, her body bowed as he nibbled at the hard little point, his hand smoothing down her abdomen, his fingers parting the lips of her sex.

"Cole. Cole, please." She was on fire, needing his touch now more than she ever had.

"Say yes," he growled as his lips moved down her body, his tongue licking sensually, then his teeth nibbling with fierce, hot nips as he parted her thighs.

"Yes," she moaned, arching against him. "Yes, Cole. Anything. Just please don't stop."

He licked a slow, long stroke through the shallow valley of her cunt, his appreciation voiced in a low, long rumbling moan. His fingers parted her, his lips covered her clit with a heated suction that had her hips jerking sharply, arching to his mouth. Her knees bent, her thighs clenching around his head as he sucked and licked at the little pearl of nerves that throbbed almost painfully.

"So good," he growled, licking at her. "Delicious, Tess. But I need more, baby. Come for me. Come for me so I can love you the way I need to."

A finger, thick and long slid deep into her vagina, his mouth covered her clit, his tongue flickering in a wicked dance of pleasure as his finger filled her, retreated, then thrust inside her again. Tess bucked against him, her legs tightening around his head, her body heaving. Fire struck her loins, swelled her clit further, clenched her womb. The blood rushed through her body, carrying ecstasy, rapture, until she felt every particle of her being erupt against his mouth.

She was still crying, arching when he jerked her thighs apart and quickly moved between them.

"I love you, Tess," he whispered as he lowered himself against her, his cock, sliding against the lips of her sex, nudging inside them, then parting the tight muscles of her vagina.

"I love you," she whispered in return as the head of his cock parted her, slid in inch by inch, easing past the sensitive tissue, allowing her to feel every hard, hot, throbbing inch he was giving her. "Oh God, Cole, you'll kill me."

It was too much. He was too slow. The exquisite stretching, the slow stroke across nerve endings so sensitive, so desperate for relief, was taking her breath. Her head tossed on the bed, her hands slid across his sweat-dampened shoulders, then clenched in the silk of his hair.

"I'm loving you," he groaned. "Enjoy it, baby, it may not happen like this again for a while."

Torturous pleasure raged through her body. She could feel the clench of her vagina on the thick, hot shaft working gently inside her, the slow stretching, the hot brand of possession as he slid in to the hilt, then paused.

"Tess, baby," he whispered as he filled her, burying his face in her neck, his lips stroking her heatedly as he groaned.

She tightened the muscles of her vagina around his cock, whimpering at the heat, the searing sensations of near orgasm.

"I love you," she cried out again, holding him close, holding him tight. "I love you Cole, but I swear to God, if you don't fuck me right now, I'll kill you."

He didn't need a second urging. Bracing his knees on the mattress, he pulled back, then slammed inside her. Tess screamed out at the rocketing, agonizing pleasure. Her back bowed, her legs curled around his hips, enclosing him in a vice as she fought to make him move harder, faster. She didn't have to urge him much.

With a harsh male cry of victory, he began to thrust heatedly, heavily inside the slick heat of her body. Tess trembled at the onslaught of fiery sensations. Her vagina was stretched, filled, repeatedly stroked in hard, long thrusts that drove her higher, closer, strangling the breath in her throat as her release began to tear through her.

Like an orgasmic quake it rushed over her body, tightened her muscles and flung her from a precipice of blistering need. Her cry echoed distantly around her as Cole gave one more gasping thrust then groaned out his release. She felt the hot, thick jets of his semen spilling inside her, filling her, completing her until she collapsed, boneless in his arms.

"Mine," he growled breathlessly. "Now that I've taken you, Tess, I won't let you go."

"Mm," she smiled tiredly. "Give me a minute and you can take me again."

Cole chuckled tiredly, rolled from her and gathered her against his sweat-dampened chest.

"Sleep first," he grunted. "Then I'll dominate you some more."

"Or I could dominate you," she suggested with a smile. "Wake you up tied down. Torture you a little."

He gave her a worried look.

"Don't worry, baby," she imitated his slow, sexy drawl. "You'll love it."

SUBMISSION

Lora Leigh

I looked up one day, and you were gone.
Your smile, your laughing eyes,
forever dimmed by death. I hadn't known
when you passed, there was no chance to lay
a rose on your grave, to whisper a tear-filled goodbye.
You were gone.
And only then did I realize the depths to
which I missed you.
Only then did I realize the regrets…

Chapter One

The house was too quiet. Ella could hear her own footfalls as she walked through it, her own heartbeat as she stared into her coffee. She could feel her fear, closer, stronger, than it had ever been before. The new house was so still, the memories that her New York home had held were absent here.

She had moved to be closer to Tess. To try in some way to make up for the cruel, bitter words she had thrown at her daughter. And she had moved to live again. She had hidden from herself and from the memories of her marriage for so many years that she was feeling the deprivation in ever increasing levels. Her family was here. Her sister, her friends. They were all here. With Tess gone, the New York house was too silent, too lonely. Though this one wasn't much different today.

She still wore the cream lace dress she had chosen for the wedding, though the matching wide brimmed hat had been thrown carelessly on the embroidered chair that sat inside the front entryway. She felt lost in a way she hadn't felt in years. A loneliness she couldn't explain haunted her; needs she couldn't admit to shadowed her mind and her desires. So she thought of Tess instead.

The wedding had been one of the most beautiful Ella had attended in her life. Her daughter, her baby, had made a gorgeous bride. The pervert she had married had looked handsome and darkly seductive.

She ran her fingers over the careful upsweep of her auburn hair, feeling the pinch of hairpins holding it in place. Her hairdresser had followed her orders to the letter. Not a strand of hair had slipped free of its mooring. Her dress hadn't creased, and her silk stockings hadn't dared slip or snag. She looked as well dressed now, six hours after the wedding, as she had when she left that morning.

Thankfully, with the move to Virginia, the damage she had done to the relationship with her daughter was healing. In her shock, in her rage, she had been hurtful to Tess. But, still, she couldn't believe what she had walked in on.

Her hands trembled as heat flooded her face. It had been Jesse, not James, but the likeness was too great. The twins were identical in nearly every way, even to their sexual preferences. Tall and distinguished, with lean, muscular builds and skin that looked perpetually tanned. Thick, black hair fell along their napes, straight and glossy, tempting the women around them to touch.

Her legs trembled as she sat down at the small, walnut kitchen table. Her fingers trembled as they covered her lips. Her heart pounded with hard, driving beats within her chest. It had been her worst nightmare come to life, except her daughter played the role Ella had played within those dark visions.

Not with Cole, but with James. And there lay the demon that lurked in her mind.

Perverse, depraved. She had walked away from her marriage and the life she had fought to build because of her husband Jase's perverse desires. The light spankings she had managed to tolerate, though they had seared her with shame. Being restrained had been easier, though even then, whatever pleasure had filtered through the experience had been tainted by the fact that she knew, knew what was coming and she knew she couldn't bear it.

Her lack of submission to Jase's needs had finally broken their relationship. She hadn't been able to give him the trust, the control he needed. She had been terrified, knowing instinctively what would come next, who would come next. And she knew she would never be able to maintain her control, her sanity, if James touched her.

He had been at Tessa's wedding. He had watched her with knowing eyes, so green, so wicked, her body had pulsed with depravity. He had shaken her hand, the heat and pleasure of his touch nearly taking her breath. And all the time he had watched her, knew her, tormented her.

She stalked to the glass door that led to the cool, foliage-sheltered area of the garden. The slender heels of her shoes created a hollow, lonely tap against the wood of the porch as she moved to the end of the vine-covered roof. Her hand gripped the thick post, her nails biting into the wood as she fought her anger, her fears for her daughter.

Tess was too much like Jase. Ella had always been afraid of that, especially after the books she had found years ago, hidden in Tess's bedroom. Her desires were extreme, and evidently she had no fear of them.

Unlike her mother, who fought the demons, the knowledge of her own needs.

She couldn't get the image of it out of her mind. She couldn't fight the dark nightmares of James, holding her, taking her as another did. She never knew, never cared who joined them in those nightmare images, all she saw, all she knew, was James.

One day, Ella, you'll have to stop running. When you do, let me know.

"Like hell," she bit out, turning and moving purposely to the house. She wasn't running, and she sure as hell wasn't going to let him know anything.

Jase's sexual tastes had nearly ruined her life, and now they would ruin Tess's. No man could truly love a woman, truly respect her, if he allowed another to touch her, to take her.

She fought the ripple of response between her thighs. The creamy moisture that she fought to ignore, the desires she kept carefully banked, always hidden. Controlled. She couldn't let him break her, couldn't let him see her response to him. If anyone had the power to break her heart, it was James Wyman.

She couldn't ignore him; she couldn't pretend he didn't exist. Due to her own foolishness, he would soon be a daily part of her life. But she could handle it, she assured herself. She had spent her life practicing the careful control that had sustained her over the years. She could handle James Wyman, easily.

It was all a matter of control.

Chapter Two

It was all a matter of control. James watched as Ella Delacourte led him up the carpet-covered stairs to the bedroom he would be using while he stayed in her home. He was still amazed that she had given into Tess's request that she allow James to stay in the house until the home he was buying was ready to move into.

Her slender waist and gently flared hips drew attention to the delicate, perfect curves of her ass as she moved in front of him. Dressed in gray silk slacks and a pearl gray blouse, she was the epitome of grace and elegance.

Calm, controlled...so perfectly controlled it made him itch to hear her scream. To hear that perfectly pitched voice ragged and hot, begging him to fuck her deep and hard, to take her however he wished. He wanted, needed, to break that control.

And Ella knew it. She had been well warned years before and he wasn't a joking man. But he was a patient man. He had waited five years for the chance at the only woman he knew that could make him think of forever. The only one he knew would challenge his mind, as well as his sexuality. If he could manage to keep from getting kicked out of the house.

He hid his grin. He knew Ella was desperate to make up for the painful words she had thrown at her daughter when she caught her sandwiched between Cole and Jesse. She had been furious, outraged, and if Jesse was right, certain at first that it was James rather than Jesse who had participated in Tess's first ménage.

Tess, too, wanted that relationship repaired, but she also wanted her mother happy. She had been more than happy to participate in James' plot to get closer to her mother. Especially after he convinced her how long he had been waiting for the opportunity.

"You can use the kitchen and the washroom if you do your own cooking and laundry. The living room is okay for entertaining, but I have to ask, that if you need overnight female companionship you rent a motel room. I won't have it in my home, James." She pushed open the bedroom door before turning to face him.

She wore only a minimum of makeup today to accentuate her eyes and her graceful cheekbones. Her lips were colored with a soft dawn shade, and at the moment the lower lip appeared slightly swollen, as though she had been biting at it as she walked upstairs.

"I'm not a teenager, Ella." He watched her carefully, aware that her blue eyes were a shade darker than normal, the pupils slightly dilated. He wondered if her pussy was wet, or if she had mastered control over even that part of her body.

"I'm aware of your age," she said coldly. "I'll leave you to get settled in. If you need anything, the house is laid out simply, and everything is easy to find. I'll talk to you later."

"Ella?" He stopped her as she turned for the door.

He caught the ready, tense set of her body, as though she were preparing herself for a battle. She turned back to him, her expression carefully closed, cool.

"Yes, James?" She kept her voice well-modulated, soft yet not simpering.

"Am I allowed to come out of my room if I'm a very good boy?" James kept his voice low, teasing. There was no way in hell he was going to get close to her if she didn't loosen up a little.

She was wary, almost frightened of him, and she almost succeeded in hiding it. Almost. He knew her better than she knew herself in some ways. She stiffened further, her perfectly arched brows snapping into a frown.

"I'm not in the mood for your games." Her voice was non-confrontational, but the flush along her cheekbones warned him of the coming storm. Damn, he loved pissing her off. Watching her eyes glitter with ire, her pale cheeks flushing so prettily. It gave him a glimpse of what she would look like in passion.

He tilted his head curiously. "Shame. Tess assured me you would welcome my company. I'm feeling as though I'm putting you out, Ella. Perhaps I should stay in a hotel until the house is ready."

For a moment—a very brief, infuriating moment—satisfaction glittered in her eyes, until she remembered Tess and her promise to make James comfortable. Her lips thinned as she drew in a deep, careful breath. The smile that she pasted on her face had little to do with warmth; it damned near caused frostbite.

"You're perfectly welcome, James. Tess's little friends are always welcome in my home, you know that."

Ouch.

Little friends? He chuckled silently.

She was finding every opportunity to remind him that he was several years younger than she was. The six years made little difference to him. As a matter of fact, it seemed perfect. An older man would never keep up with the passions he knew ran beneath that cool exterior.

He allowed a smile to curve his lips as he stared at her intently. "Little friends? I'm hardly that young, Ella."

"Not far from it," she grumbled. "I have work to do, James. Make yourself at home, and perhaps I'll talk to you later."

But not if she could help it.

"What type of work?" He stopped her again. "I was unaware you worked. Jase should have given you a very healthy settlement from the divorce."

By God, if he hadn't, James would be talking to him about it.

"That's none of your business." She frowned again. "What I do, James, I do for my own pleasure, and how Jase decided to pay me for the divorce is none of your concern."

Pay her for the divorce? James was damned well aware that she was much less than happy in that marriage, yet she sounded bitter, rejected. Had she cared more for Jase than he had once thought? That idea didn't set well in his mind, or in his heart.

"Ella, you weren't happy, and neither was Jase," he said softly.

"I refuse to discuss this with you." She straightened her shoulders majestically, her lips thinning as her anger grew. "I don't mind your presence here, James, but I don't have time to entertain you. You'll have to find your amusements elsewhere."

"But you said no women," he reminded her.

She stopped again as she turned to leave.

"No women." She shook her head tightly, her voice strained. "Not in my home, James. Never again in my home."

Chapter Three

"You know, you need a housekeeper or a cook."

James's voice early the next afternoon had her jumping in startled awareness as she finished filling the coffeepot. She turned, facing him, thinking what a shame it was that one man would have such sexual presence.

He stood propped against the doorway, dressed in dark blue silk slacks and a lighter blue silk shirt. His jacket was held at his shoulder by the crook of his finger, and his green eyes regarded her with lustful secrets.

"I'm perfectly capable of cooking my own meals and cleaning my home." She had been raised to do for herself, and cleaning gave her something to do, a way to occupy her hands when her body was filled with restless energy.

He straightened from the doorframe, walking to the table with a casual male grace that threatened to take her breath. She turned quickly from him, moving to the cabinet to retrieve her coffee cup. She fought to still her shaking hands, the nervousness in her stomach that wouldn't go away. She felt immature, like a quaking child before him. It was… unbalancing.

"What if you became busy? Or found a lover?"

Ella fought back her panic. She felt aged, past the time when she could have worried about the future, or a man in her life.

"I'm not looking for a lover, James." She poured her coffee, moving with what she hoped was casual unconcern to the work isle in the center of the room.

She leaned her hip against it, lowering her head as she concentrated on stirring cream and sugar into the dark liquid. She was aware that he was watching her, his eyes dark, intent. She was well aware of his desire for her; a desire she knew wouldn't last beyond the moment. She had no illusions about herself. She was growing older, and her body was slowly showing the signs of it. It wasn't something she worried much about, until she was faced with James. He made her feel young, made her feel desired, and it was dangerous to allow herself to be convinced that it could go further. Too dangerous for her heart.

She watched as he laid the jacket over the back of a chair then moved to the cabinet and snagged a cup for himself. His arm reached up, muscles bunching in his shoulders and back. She shivered, her hands itching to touch him, to feel the strength of motion beneath his flesh.

He turned back to her, leaning against the counter as he regarded her quizzically. "Do you have a lover?"

His voice was whisky-rough and dark. It caused arousal to zip along her nerve endings, her skin to become sensitive, needy for his touch. She hated it.

"That's really none of your business." She fought to stay in control. He would leave soon; she knew Jase depended on him at the corporate offices. Not that she understood any of the legal talk she had ever heard in the past, but his job, she knew, was complicated and often required late nights and full days. She was hoping that would keep him out of her hair for the most part.

"Maybe I want to make it my business." His voice hardened imperceptibly as he watched her, his gaze brooding.

Ella couldn't stop the surprise that she knew was reflected on her face. She blinked over at him, her chest tightening in unwanted excitement, her vagina throbbing in unwanted preparation for his touch.

"Why would you want to?" She couldn't understand his desire for her in any way. "I'm not in the market for complications, James. A lover is, by his very nature, a complication."

He tilted his head, his lips quirking in amusement as she raised the coffee cup to her lips.

"Don't you ever get horny, Ella?" She nearly dropped the cup. The coffee she had just taken into her mouth threatened to choke her as it went down the wrong way.

She wheezed, her eyes widening, tearing as she stared at him in shock.

"For God's sake," she bit out when she could breathe again. "Is that any of your business, in any way, James?"

"Actually, it is." He shrugged his shoulders with deceptive laziness. "I want you, Ella. I want to lay you down and touch you in all the ways a man can. I want to fuck you until you're screaming, because it feels so damned good it hurts. So yeah." He nodded. "It's my business."

The breath lodged in her throat. She felt her pussy cream, her thighs tremble at the thought of him powering into her, fucking her as she screamed. She had never screamed, never wanted anything desperately enough to beg. But she couldn't have James.

Anger, directed at herself, at him, poured through her.

She felt her face flush, her body tremble, as she fought for control.

"Sorry, James." She smiled tightly. "I'm really not in the market for a boy toy this year. I guess you're just out of luck there."

She didn't give him time to reply. Before he could cut her down, before he could tempt her further, she swept from the room, rushing to the safety of her bedroom where her control wasn't as important. Where it wouldn't matter if the tears that filled her eyes escaped. All that mattered was that James didn't know.

Chapter Four

She wouldn't survive this. Ella escaped to her bedroom, locked the door clumsily behind her and stood against it, breathing raggedly. She was flushed, heated, her body tingling. She hated it.

Her fists clenched as she felt her vagina spasm, growing wetter by the second as she remembered the sound of his dark, velvet voice. The deep baritone stroked over her senses, then plunged heatedly into her womb. How was she supposed to maintain her control this way? She despised the person she had been while married to Jase. She had acted like a harpy, her fury and fears driving her to rages that had terrified her.

For years. Years she had fought him and what he wanted from her. Because she had known how much he wanted from her. The sexual excesses he enjoyed. She pressed her fists to her stomach, fighting the driving, insidious images that pounded at her brain. She could have tolerated it, she told herself. She could have allowed herself to let go if she hadn't known the man who would eventually arrive.

Jase was nothing if not honest. He had never lied to her when his sexuality had begun emerging. They had been in their early twenties, and his need to dominate, to control her sexual responses, had at first seemed merely harmless play. He hated her controlled sexuality. Her fear of letting go, of giving him the responsibility of pleasing her.

Ella had hated his need for it. She had married him because she was pregnant. She had cared for him, had felt a warmth and gentle desire for him, but what he needed she had never wanted. Until she met James. Until she saw in his wicked, knowing eyes, the truth about herself.

God, he had been twenty-six, and she was already in her thirties. She had felt like a cradle robber, looking at him, feeling her pussy gush with moisture, her breasts swelling in desire. And then, she had begun to fantasize. When Jase took her, his cock burrowing into her as he held her to the bed, she imagined it was James.

When he tied her to the bed, her nipples would bead instantly as she thought of James tying her down, thought of James tormenting her body, driving her ragged with need. And when Jase had suggested a ménage, she had thought of James, yet still pretended her husband wasn't truly serious.

Until the day James had walked into the room Jase had set up for his play. She had been tied to the narrow bed, her legs gaping, as Jase grew more and more frustrated over her lack of response. James had walked in, his brilliant eyes going to her smooth, bare pussy and she had creamed instantly. She had fought Jase, vowing to never allow him to touch her again. The screaming match that ensued lasted for years. Until the divorce.

She couldn't stand it. For years she had pushed her own needs back, fought to forget James and the terrible desires that raged through her system. Until she walked in and saw Tess with Jesse, James's twin brother. Betrayal had sliced through her soul. And Jesse, damn his black heart, had known. She had seen it in his eyes, in the sardonic lift of his mouth.

Her hand raised to one throbbing breast as the ache in her nipples seemed only to grow. Her fingers glanced over the hard point beneath the silk blouse and sheer bra she wore. Her breath caught on a gasp at the electrified pleasure that washed over her.

She felt her pussy cream furiously, spilling the thick essence along her bare foldss. Jase had started her habit of shaving there. It was one of the few things he had taught her that she was thankful for. Until now. Now, the incredible sensitivity of her bare inner lips was a curse. She could feel her juices, hot and slick, coating her flesh as they eased from her vagina, and it only made her ache more.

How was she going to bear having him in her house? Her arms wrapped around her waist as her womb clenched. He hadn't been here an hour yet and already she could think of nothing but his touch moving over her, his hands stroking her, spanking her... She whimpered. She didn't want that, she cried silently, couldn't bear it.

"Ella, you in there? I'm ordering lunch, how do you feel about pizza?" He knocked on her door, startling her into jumping away from it with a tight gasp.

God, wasn't he ever going to leave for work? Surely he wouldn't be here for lunch. She couldn't handle it.

"Fine." She was horrified at the husky, needy quality of her voice. She cleared her throat and swallowed tightly. "I'm tired. You eat. I'm going to lie down."

"Ella, come out and talk to me," he cajoled, his voice soft, filled with such wicked promises she had to bite her lip to keep from calling him to her. "It's just pizza, nothing else." Amusement was like a dark vein of sin in his tone.

She glanced at the clock, then the bedside window. She could find no reasonable excuse to stay hidden in her room, and she knew if she continued to refuse it would only make him suspicious.

"Fine," she bit out, feeling her nails piercing the skin of her palms. "I'll be out in a while. I need to freshen up first."

"I'll be waiting on you. Don't take too long."

As he spoke, Ella tore desperately at her clothes to remove them. She was too hot, too aroused, to go to him like this. If she didn't find relief, no matter how minute, she would burn in flames of desire if he so much as brushed against her.

She jerked the drawer of her bedside table open and pulled out the slender, slim line vibrator she had purchased years ago. The soft, supple latex flexed in her palm as she stretched out on her bed. It wasn't thick or long, but buying the damned thing had been one of the hardest things she had ever done in her life.

Her body was already primed, her cunt so wet and sticky that when she ran her fingers through the narrow slit, it clung to her fingers. Her clit was swollen, so large and sensitive she gasped as she circled it with the head of the slender dildo. She eased the control switch on the vibration up, shuddering as the device began to hum.

She couldn't still her gasp of breath as she slid it into the hungry opening of her pussy. Her muscles closed on it, relishing in the hum, but still greedy for more. She pushed it deeper, feeling the sensitive tissue part for the invader.

Ella writhed on the bed, her eyes clenched tightly closed as the fingers of her other hand gripped one of her tight, elongated nipples and pinched lightly.

She couldn't groan, she told herself. She couldn't cry out his name as she had done since seeing him at the wedding and agreeing to let him stay. She couldn't pretend it was James pushing inside her wet pussy, fucking her tight depths. But she couldn't help it either. Her mind formed the image. His body hard and muscular, his cock thick and long as it pushed inside her.

Her control weakened as a small whimper escaped her throat. It wasn't going to be enough. Oh God, she could feel it, the weakness of her body, the incredible arousal searing her nerve endings.

She would never achieve a climax hard enough to still the raging pain.

"Let me help you, Ella." The words were like a splash of cold water.

Her eyes flew open to see James, fully dressed, his green eyes glowing with lust as he stared down at her nude, perspiring body. From her breasts to her still slender thighs, spread invitingly as she moved the vibrating dildo inside her pussy.

"Oh God." Embarrassment washed over her as she realized he really was standing there, watching her. He was real this time, not a figment of her imagination.

She would have jumped from the bed if James hadn't moved to stop her, pinning her shoulders to the mattress as he forced her legs closed, holding the vibrator inside her pussy as he stared down at her, his powerful legs clamped on the outside of hers as she stared up at him in horror.

His eyes were dark, wicked, his expression filled with sensuality, with lust. Her legs were clamped together as his fingers moved to the control box at her side and he thumbed the power up to its highest level.

Her body jerked in response as the heat flared higher, hotter inside her tormented depths.

"Who do you imagine inside you, Ella?" His voice was deep, rough. "Who's fucking that tight pussy for you, in your mind?"

The deep baritone of his voice stroked over her nerve endings, sending her senses into overdrive.

Her hips jerked in reflex, her clit pulsing, throbbing in reaction.

"Don't do this," she cried out, fighting the pleasure as he forced her wrists into one broad hand, holding her securely as he stared into her eyes.

"Is it me, Ella?" he asked her softly. "Do I fuck you in your fantasies? I sure as hell fuck you in mine. Hard and deep. But my cock is a hell of a lot thicker than that baby pecker you picked. When I push inside you, you're going to be so damned tight you'll come from the pleasure/pain alone. Come for me now, Ella. Come for me baby, so we can discuss this rationally."

Ella couldn't bear it. His voice was enough to make her juices flood her pussy, making the vibration echo along her sensitized flesh.

"I can't." She fought to hold onto her control. She couldn't do this. It was too horrifying, too humiliating. Dear God, how had he opened a locked door?

He leaned closer, his legs loosening from around hers, his hand moving between their bodies as he watched her. She twisted against him as he forced his hand between her slick thighs and gripped the end of the dildo.

"I'm going to fuck you, Ella." He pulled it back as she cried out, staring up at him, seeing his grimace of hot, desperate lust. "Like this." The vibrator was thrust into her pussy, squishing through the thick juices, pounding into her womb as he began to fuck her hard and fast with her own toy.

Her eyes widened. Her body stiffened as ripples of electricity began to flare through her womb. She could have survived it. She fought for control and it was nearly in her grasp when his head lowered to her nipples.

It had been nearly a decade since a man had touched her. Nearly ten years of fantasizing about this, aching and dreaming of his dominant touch. When his teeth gripped her nipple, his tongue rasping over it as he fucked the vibrator hard and deep inside her pussy, she lost all sense of control.

An orgasm unlike anything she had ever known ripped through her body. She felt the juices spray from her pussy as James groaned, fucking her harder with the latex toy, pushing her thighs apart and heading for her clit. When his lips covered it, his tongue stroked it, she screamed. Her hips arched, her pussy greedily sucking at the vibrator as her clit exploded, and she was flung into a vortex of pleasure that horrified her with its force.

It wouldn't stop. Her upper body jerked from the bed as her muscles contracted, her pussy exploding so hard, so deep, every bone and muscle spasmed in response. She shuddered, feeling the muscles tightening on the vibration inside her as she shook in the grip of her orgasm.

Moments, hours, later she collapsed to the bed again, though her womb continued to contract in deep, hard surges as the thick cream flowed from between her thighs.

"There, baby," James soothed her gently and she realized she was crying. His lips feathered over her cheek as he slowly lowered the speed of the vibrator, bringing her back to sanity. She could smell the slight earthy scent of her pussy on his lips, and shuddered at the knowledge of it. "It's okay, baby," he whispered again. "Come back to me, Ella. It's okay now." He eased back to look at her as the tears welled from her eyes and poured down her cheeks. "Don't cry, Ella," he whispered gently. "It's okay, baby, it's what we both needed for now."

She shook her head, fighting now to be free of him, to remove the proof of her need, of her own perversions, from the dripping channel between her thighs. She rolled to her side to escape him, but before she could get away, he pushed her down again, on her stomach, the vibrator once again trapped inside her quaking flesh.

"No, Ella." His voice was hard, tight with lust as his hand smoothed over the quivering cheeks of her rear. "You won't run from it, and by God, I won't let you hide from it any longer." His fingers ran down the cleft of her ass as he hummed in approval.

The juices that flowed from her pussy had slicked the area, giving his fingers greater ease despite the tightening of her muscles.

"James. No," she cried out as he circled the tight opening of her anus. Horror and shame streaked through her system, because despite her embarrassment, she could feel the entrance relaxing, her betraying body sucking at the tip of his finger.

"For now." He was breathing hard at her ear, his chest laboring under his breaths. "For now, Ella. I'll leave you, this time. But you have fifteen minutes to bring that pretty ass out to the living room where we can discuss this with relative sanity. You will not run, Ella. You will not hide. You've come in my mouth now and I'll be damned, but I won't wait much longer to feel you coming around my cock. Fifteen minutes."

He moved quickly from her, stalking to the door. "And the next fucking time you try to lock a door against me, I'll break the son of a bitch down. Fifteen minutes."

CHAPTER FIVE

James was shaking as he stalked to the pristine, perfectly organized living room. His hands, his entire body, were nearly shuddering in lust and need, and he feared the loss of his own control.

Never.

In his entire sexual life his own control had never been so sorely tempted as it had been in Ella's bed, watching her push that pitiful excuse for a dildo inside her tight pussy.

The vibrating toy was slender, soft to the touch, a teaser. A toy to use to drive her to distraction and make her hungry for more, and she didn't even know it. But he intended to do his best to instruct her on the best toys for the job. The job of preparing her, opening her, driving her insane for his final possession.

Jerking the cell phone from his waistband he made a quick call. His eyes watched the door carefully as he put in the order to the online supplier of adult products. A collection of toys, of devices, and he alone would show her the proper use of them.

He wouldn't have long. It would take her five minutes, he guessed, to work herself up. Another five to struggle back into her clothing as she fought the lethargy of her orgasm. Damn. He shook his head as he gave the owner of the adult products store the list. Damn, she had climaxed like nothing he had ever seen. Her pussy had gripped that dildo so tight, so hard, he'd had to struggle to fuck her through the rippling pleasure.

He had watched her abdomen, seeing the convulsive shudders of her womb beneath her flesh as she cried out his name. But she hadn't screamed it, and he swore before the week was over, she was going to scream his name.

He had just ended the call and pushed the phone back into its holder when she stormed into the room.

"You dirty son of a bitch!" she screamed with rage and fear. "You dirty, perverted bastard. This is my home. Mine. And you can fucking leave now."

No control. She flew at him, her face flushed, murder in her eyes, intent on knocking the hell out of him. He didn't think so. He had seen that bruise Jase had sported for a week, years before their divorce.

Before she could land the blow he grabbed her wrists, shackling them together in one hand behind her back. His arm went around her waist and he jerked her against him. Before she could curse him again, his lips slanted over hers.

She bit at him, but he nipped at her lip warningly a second before his tongue plunged into her mouth. She was heat and anger, and desperate, hungry lust.

She groaned into the kiss, fighting his hold though her lips opened for his tongue, then suckled it tight into her mouth.

James groaned, his cock jerking beneath his zipper at the thought of her mouth enclosing it in such hot pleasure. But for now, his mouth had her, and the taste of her was indescribable. Sweet and warm, filled with the heady, aroused whimpers of a woman overcome with her own desires, pleasured, hungry for more.

He allowed his tongue to stroke the inside of her mouth, to twine with hers as his head slanted, angling closer to allow his lips to stroke hers. She was trembling in his arms, and he knew her pussy would be dripping, wet and aching. And tight. He groaned at the thought of that as he lifted her closer. She had been so tight on that damned slender vibrator that he could barely fuck her with it. She would strangle his cock. His body tensed, his tongue fucking her mouth as she growled with greedy passion beneath his kiss.

He couldn't get enough of her. She arched to him, her breasts unconfined beneath the loose silk shirt she wore, her pants-covered thighs plastered to his as she pressed her mound hard against the thick erection beneath his slacks. The soft cotton pants she wore would do her little good, he promised himself. She would soak them with the juices from her sweet little cunt just as she had the silk slacks.

With a muttered groan he pulled back from the kiss and stared into her face. Her eyes were dazed, her expression slack with sensual need. He could have her now if he was willing to take her. To give her no time for thought, to allow her to believe he had forced the control from her as he had in the bedroom. That would only hurt his intent. It would do nothing to further his own personal goals.

"Enough," he growled, holding onto her as he pushed her into the recliner at his side. "Sit there. And don't get up, Ella, or I promise, you'll regret it," he warned her as she made to do just that.

Evidently she heard the strain of his own fight for control in his voice. She pressed herself tighter against the back of the chair, staring up at him with wide eyes.

James drew in a tight breath. His cock throbbed beneath his pants, pleading for a touch, no matter how timid, no matter how forced. He gritted his teeth and moved back from her.

"Ten years," he bit out, watching her broodingly. "I've wanted you for ten years, Ella, and I'm tired of fighting it."

She shook her head, shock darkening her eyes. "That's not possible." Her voice was thready, desperate.

"Oh, it's more than possible." Disgust welled inside him. "I've wanted you until I could barely breathe, ever since I walked into that damned house of Jase's and saw all that careful control as you fought to give him at least part of what he wanted."

Her face flamed and her eyes looked wild.

"Did you think I couldn't see who you were, Ella? Every time I saw you, you watched me as though you were terrified. Your nipples would harden, your face would flush, and I knew you wanted me. Me, Ella. And I fought it, fought it just as fucking hard as you did until I walked into that playroom."

He remembered it clearly. Seeing her strapped down on the cot, unaroused, but trying, as Jase fought to pleasure her. He had seen her small cunt; dry yet looking so soft, so tender, as Jase touched it. Then she had seen him. She had fought Jase, screaming at him, crying, but James had watched those soft folds, mesmerized. And within seconds it had glistened, her juices spreading over the delicate lips.

He'd left. Turned and stalked from the room because he couldn't stand to see her lying there, crying brokenly as she cursed her husband. Jase had given up. He hadn't loved her, and James knew it. What he needed sexually drove him, until he began to bring other women to his bed as his wife moved to the solitary comfort of a downstairs bedroom.

Never in my home. Never again, she had said earlier. He had seen the humiliation flash in her gaze. Jase had brought other women to her home, had taken them to his bed, destroying the pride that was so much a part of her.

"I want you to leave." Her voice quivered as she crossed her arms beneath her breasts, refusing to look at him. "I want you to leave now."

James snorted. "Do you enjoy wasting your breath, Ella? You don't want me to leave. You're just too fucking scared for me to stay."

"No." She shook her head desperately.

"Yes," he all but snarled. "Prove it then. Stand up, Ella, and drop those pants. Let me sink my fingers into that tight cunt and see if you're still wet and ready for me, because I bet you are. I bet you would come again, Ella..."

"Stop it." She jerked to her feet, her voice raspy, hoarse. "You're younger..."

"I'll fuck you harder than any man your own age could ever hope to." He stood in front of her, staring down at her furiously. "Better yet, Ella, I'll fuck you like you need it. I'll make all your nasty little fantasies come true, and then I'll teach you some you could have never imagined."

"I won't listen to this," she raged heatedly. "I let you come into my house as a guest..."

"And I'll come in your pussy as your lover," he bit out, breaking over her outraged declaration. "Your pussy, your mouth, your ass. Wherever I can get my cock in, Ella, I'll fuck you until I can fill every inch of your body with my cum."

She collapsed back in the chair. He could see her trembling, fighting herself as well as him.

"But we both know it's not that easy, don't we, baby?" He stooped in front of her, his hands going to the button of her pants. "We both know that what I want will be more intense, and a hell of a lot more serious than anything Jase ever asked of you, and that's what's scaring the hell out of you."

"James." Her hand covered his as her voice broke. "Don't do this to me, please."

"Don't do what, Ella?" he asked her, tenderness—fuck, love—welling inside him so deep, so strong it nearly strangled him. "Don't give you what you need? Don't satisfy your fantasies, your desires? Don't show you how damned good it's going to hurt when my cock pushes inside your tight pussy? Sorry, baby, but I think I just reached the end of my control. I won't let you run anymore."

⚜ ⚜ ⚜

Ella watched James, seeing the determination in his eyes, the lust that flushed his face, tightened his features, and she couldn't find the words to fight him. She trembled before him instead, her body still weak, still vibrating in longing after the climax he had given her earlier. She needed more. Her thighs trembled, her cunt gushing her juices as she tried to find a way to make him leave.

She could make him. She could call the police and he wouldn't stop her. She could have him thrown out. She could scream if she could find the breath for it after that kiss. But she knew she couldn't bear to see him dragged away. Couldn't bear the humiliation she knew he would face. But she couldn't give in to him either. She wouldn't give in to him. At least, not entirely.

"Just us," she finally whispered, trembling. "Just sex."

His whole body tightened. She had expected him to finish removing her pants, to give her what she needed. She didn't expect him to draw away from her.

"I take control," he said broodingly. "Whatever I want to give you, Ella, however I want to give it."

"My terms," she bit out desperately, then watched in horror as he shook his head slowly.

"No, Ella. My terms as my woman. Your choice."

Chapter Six

My terms as my woman. Your choice.

The words resounded in her head that night and all the next day.

James was the head corporate lawyer for Delacourte Electronics, and with the growth of Jase's business, she knew he often put in long hours working, both in the office and at home, she guessed. That left the house silent and lonely that next day.

She wandered through the rooms, tired from the restlessness of her sleep the night before and torn between her desires and his. She remembered clearly Jase's demented sexual games. Not that any of them made sense to her at the time. What was the purpose in tying a woman down? Unless your fantasy was rape, which he always swore wasn't true. She hadn't had a clue until James walked into that damned room and stared with flaring lust at her naked, bound body.

Ella remembered, clearly, her own agonizing humiliation. Spread open while her husband touched her, as she fought to find arousal in the game he wanted to play. But there had been none.

Nothing until James's eyes had centered on her thighs, spearing past her boredom with an instant, flaring heat. She had creamed herself in seconds and the terror that Jase, or even James, would realize it, had nearly destroyed her.

She sighed morosely as she walked out to the back porch and threw herself into one of the padded loungers there. The late afternoon sun was passing over, but beneath the cool shelter of the low trees and thick vines that wrapped around the porch, Ella was spared the blinding heat. The outer heat. Her inner heat was killing her.

She had finally given up on changing panties. After the second pair, she had thrown her hands up in disgust and stopped. After ten years of no sexual activity, of fighting her desires and her needs, her body was evidently taking over. It wouldn't stop producing the hot, slick fluid that would ease James's entrance into her tight pussy. And it was tight. She shuddered in longing. Tight and greedy, anxious to feel James's thick, hard cock sliding into it.

She was losing her mind. She closed her eyes as she tightened her thighs against the empty ache in the center of her body. Her vibrator had disappeared. She didn't know how, or why, but somehow James had managed to steal it, or hide it, because it was no place to be found. And she needed it.

"You look pretty there, Ella." She jolted as James stepped to the doorway, staring at her with those hot, sin-filled eyes.

"What are you doing here? You're supposed to be working." She would have jumped from the lounge chair if he hadn't moved to stand in front of it.

She stared up at him, fighting to control her breathing as well as the desire that shook her to her soul.

"I took the rest of the day off." He shrugged his broad shoulders as he pushed his hands into the pockets of his pants. The action only drew attention to the thick ridge beneath the material. "Is your pussy wet?"

Ella blinked as the question took her by surprise.

"Are you insane?" her voice squeaked in shock.

"Most likely," he growled. "Make me crazier. It's your chance for revenge, Ella. Tell me how wet your pussy is."

She bit her lip, breathing fast and hard as she seriously considered the request.

"Go back to work," she finally whispered desperately, shaking her head.

"Ella, remember how nice I was to you yesterday when my mouth sucked that sweet little clit of yours?"

How could she forget?

"I didn't ask you to break into my room, James."

"I want you to suck my cock like that, Ella. While you're tied belly down on my bed, my cock thrusting slow and easy in your mouth and I inflate the plug I'm going to push up your sweet, virgin ass."

"Stop. Why are you doing this to me?" Her pussy was gushing between her thighs, so hot it felt blistered by her need. "For God's sake, James, surely you can find someone to fuck. Do you have to torture me this way?"

She pushed her fingers through her loose hair, feeling the silky strands brush her shoulders, almost shivering at the caress against her ultra-sensitive flesh. She was being driven crazy, and he knew it. Maybe it was some kind of messed up mid-life crisis, she thought desperately. Because she knew her own arousal had never tormented her to this degree. It was hell and she wanted it to stop. She wanted him to leave. Or did she?

"I won't waste my breath answering that question," he bit out as he stooped down at the end of the lounger. "You want to control it, Ella? Do you really think you can?"

He was so handsome he broke her heart. Hard and toned, his body muscular and so filled with male grace that it took her breath every time she looked at him. And his face, arrogant with just a touch of the aristocratic in his strong, straight nose and superior expression.

"James, I'm asking you to stop this." Her heart was racing out of control. How was she supposed to deny him when her body ached so desperately for him?

He was like a fever in her blood. As long as she stayed away from him, she could survive it. But now, with his desire for her so clear, her needs raging through her body, she couldn't find the will to resist him. She was weak. She admitted it and she hated it. Hated the emotional and physical responses that she couldn't fight any longer.

"Lie back for me, Ella," he whispered softly. "Lie back, and let me show you what I can do for you."

Ella watched him helplessly. Her body was tense, demanding action. Demanding that she do as he ask and lie back in the lounger for him. She watched as his tongue touched his sensual lips, as though anticipating a meal, and she knew what he wanted. Knew what he would do to her. Her pussy gushed in response.

She whimpered as he moved, his hands reaching for her arms, pulling them gently, taking the support she used to keep her body upright as he released the back of the lounger. He lowered her until her back rested on the flat surface.

Ella stared up at him, trembling, hating the weakness that flooded her body. Damn him. He was so assured, so sensual, so damned tempting she could barely keep her senses intact.

"James." Her breath caught in arousal as his fingers went to the tiny buttons of her bodice. Her breasts were unbound beneath the fabric, her nipples hard, on fire for his touch.

"I've dreamed of touching you, Ella," he whispered, his green eyes darkening, the thick black lashes lowering sensually over the wicked orbs. "Ached to taste you. Do you have any idea the hell I've gone through for the last ten years, wanting to hear you scream my name as you climax for me?"

A whimper escaped her lips as the last button of the dress came free, and he was able to spread the edges apart with slow deliberation. Her body was laid out before him then, only the thin silk of her panties left to cover the front of her body.

"You're wet for me, Ella," he whispered, his eyes centering on the pale green triangle of fabric. "And you still shave your pretty pussy, don't you? When my tongue caresses it, laps up all that thick cream, you'll feel every soft touch, won't you?"

His hand spread her legs slowly. Ella gripped the sides of the lounger, watching him, mesmerized by the sensuality in his expression, the hunger reflected in his eyes, in the curve of his lips.

"James." She whispered his name, her voice rough, pleading as she caught his hands when they moved to the band of her panties. "I can't..." She couldn't finish the sentence, couldn't force the words past her lips.

"Can't what, baby?" he asked her gently, his fingers hooking in the elastic, pulling her panties down, away from her weak grip. "Can't lie back and feel good for me? Can't see if what we've waited for all these years isn't as good as what we've imagined? Why can't you do that?"

He was hypnotizing her, she thought desperately. Stealing her will with the sound of his deep, rough voice. Making her crazy for him with that dark, hooded look.

She trembled as he removed the scrap of silk then spread her legs wider. All the while he watched her from the side of the lounger, his chest moving hard and fast, as he seemed to fight for breath himself, his eyes darkening lustfully.

"Damn, Ella, you're prettier than I ever imagined." His hand moved up her thigh until his fingers grazed the desperate heat and thick juices that coated her pussy. The proof of her weakness. The proof that she was just as depraved, just as perverted as Jase had been, because she knew, knew beyond a shadow of a doubt exactly what James wanted from her.

"I can't." She jerked from him, moving before he could stop her, stumbling from the lounger then rushing desperately away from him. Away from her own needs.

Chapter Seven

She rushed to her bedroom, fighting her tears, her fears. James's voice was dark, angry behind her, spurring her forward, making her heart beat in dread. If he touched her again, asked her again, she wouldn't be able to refuse him. He was her weakness. He was her sin. She slammed the door behind her, then fought to drag the suitcase from her closet. If he wouldn't leave, then she would. He could have the fucking house. Do whatever the hell he wanted. She couldn't stand it anymore. She ignored her dress as it flared away from the front of her body, ignored her nakedness beneath it. She had to leave, had to get away from him.

Bent over, her mind centered on pulling the damned case from the small utility closet, she was unaware that James had followed her until he burst into the bedroom, gripped her hips and tossed her on the bed.

"Damn you," she screeched as she came to her knees, clutching the sides of her dress. Her eyes widened as she watched him undress. Slowly. Watching her with narrowed, intent eyes.

The air in the bedroom heated, thinned, until she had to fight for breath. She sat on her knees, gripping the edges of her dress together, fighting just to breathe as each article of clothing was dropped to the floor, until he wore nothing but his own brazen sexuality.

Dear God. He was naked. All dark, sleek skin and toned muscle. Especially the bulging length of his cock. It was thick and hard, the head flared and appearing bruised, it was so engorged with blood. She couldn't take her eyes from it, couldn't stop the whimper that escaped her lips.

"First lesson," he growled dominantly, his voice brooking no refusal. "Take your dress off and lay down on the bed."

"Are you insane?" She repeated her earlier question.

"Most likely," he bit out, his hand going to the engorged flesh rising between his thighs. She watched, mesmerized, as his fingers stroked the hard cock. "So it might be best to placate me."

She licked her lips. "What are you going to do?"

He walked over to the dresser and picked up the articles she hadn't seen until then. He must have placed them there before coming to her on the back porch.

The first looked like a slender cock, the middle thinner than the flared head, with a hose and bulb leading from the base. With it was a small tube of gel lubrication. In the other hand, he picked up the leather wrist and ankle restraints. Her eyes widened.

"I'm going to fuck your ass, eventually," he told her softly. "While I'm fucking your sweet mouth and your tight little pussy, I'm going to be preparing your ass to take me. The inflatable plug will take care of that."

Inflatable? How much did it inflate? It already looked too damned big to her.

"James, please." She shook her head, reduced to pleading. "Don't do this to me. I don't think I can bear it."

Physically she was dying for it, emotionally, she was terrified.

"We'll start out easy." He wasn't asking her, he was demanding. "Undress and lie on the bed."

"Why?" She couldn't take her eyes off the restraints. "Why do you have to tie me down?"

He laid everything at the bottom of the bed. "It's all about control." He eased the straps of her sundress from her shoulders. "The one losing it, the one possessing it. My pleasure, Ella, comes from yours. But you think you have to control that pleasure. Fight it. I want you restrained, unable to run from me, unable to fight what I need to give you. I want you to lose that control that keeps you locked inside your own fears." She trembled as the material of her dress skimmed her swollen breasts.

"I don't like it," she whispered, almost groaning as his lips feathered her shoulder.

"If your pussy doesn't get wet and hot for me, if your body doesn't scream out for more, then I'll stop. I'll know if it's not right for you." The dress fell to the bed behind her. "Now, lie down for me, on your stomach first."

Ella licked her lips. God, she wanted him. She had controlled it with Jase, no matter the fantasies of James that had tormented her. Surely she could control her heart, if nothing else.

Shaken, weakened by her own desires, her own fantasies, she did as he ordered.

"Have you ever been taken anally, Ella?" he asked her then. "Not a plug, but by Jase, or anyone else?"

She shook her head, careful to keep her face buried in the blankets of the bed. He attached the leather restraints to her legs first, the small links of the chains rattling as he secured them to the short bedposts. He moved then to her wrists. His hands were gentle, caressing, the leather cool as he secured it above each hand before securing the chains to the headboard.

She was spread out. Though there was some slack in the chains, she wouldn't be able to go far if she did move. She shuddered, dragging in air with a sense of desperation as her arousal intensified. Never with Jase had she felt the trepidation and searing desire that she did now. As though she had known Jase was no threat to her, either emotionally or sexually, but James was. He could destroy her. If she let him.

"So nice," he whispered as he moved back to the bottom of the bed, moving between her spread thighs.

His hands ran up the backs of her thighs as she trembled beneath his touch. They were long-fingered and broad, warm and slightly calloused, creating an exciting friction on her flesh.

"I used to hide and watch you whenever I saw you out in public," he whispered. "I knew you would run if you saw me, and I loved watching you move, Ella. Watching the sweet curves of your ass flex, the line of your back, the tilt of your head. I'd drink in the sight of you."

Ella's hands clenched in the blankets beneath her as his hands cupped the lower curves of her rear, spreading her apart sensually. She could feel her inner flesh, drenched and hot, rippling with convulsive shudders of need. She couldn't stop the involuntary flexing of her buttocks, or the little whimper that escaped her throat.

"Are you comfortable?" he asked her, his voice low, rough.

"No." She had to fight for air. She felt intoxicated and yet on the edge of panic.

"Good." He patted her rear a little sharply in approval. Ella flinched at the tingling heat that washed up her spine from the light tap. "Now, I want you to try to relax for me a little, Ella. I want to put the plug inside you, get you ready, before we go any further."

Relax? He was kidding, she thought. He had to be.

She felt him moving at the bottom of the bed, his body shifting beneath her before his hair brushed her leg. She jerked as his hands went under her thighs, lifting her a bit before his tongue thrust hard and fast inside the soaked channel of her pussy.

"Oh God! James!" she cried out, her back bowing in reflex, angling her hips higher for the invasion.

His tongue was like a flame, searing her vagina as he pushed in hard, then pulled back slowly. As though he had already shaken the foundations of her desire, he began to lap at her. His tongue licked and stroked, drawing her juices from her body as he murmured his appreciation of her taste, or her need, she wasn't certain.

His fingers moved to the gentle curve of her inner lips, spreading them marginally as his tongue delved higher, licking through the slit, circling her clit. Teasing strokes of his demon tongue had her grinding her pussy into his mouth, and yet with little ease. As she moved closer, his mouth drew farther away.

She was only barely aware of his fingers probing between her buttocks, slick with the cool gel of the lubrication that coated them. One long finger pierced her puckered opening as James's tongue speared deep inside her vagina once again.

Ella's eyes flew open as a gasp escaped her lips. Braced only partially on her knees, the slack in the restraints taken up by her position, there was no way to escape the invasion. She moaned, a drawn-out sound of shocked pleasure, heated pain, as his tongue fucked her clenching vagina once again.

"James," she whimpered, fighting to hold onto her control.

Her anus stretched around the probing finger, welcoming the heated sensations that came from his smooth, stroking movements. He didn't answer her unspoken plea, one she wasn't certain of herself; rather he pulled the finger back, added another and pushed into the tight entrance once again.

A strangled cry escaped Ella's throat.

"Easy, darlin'." His voice was a rough croon as his fingers began to gently scissor inside her anus, stretching her slowly as he slurped at the juices running from her heated pussy.

The bite of pain was intoxicating, addicting. Pleasure swelled inside her as he stretched her, licked her, his other hand moving up her body until it tucked beneath her breast, his fingers plucking at her nipple. She was shaking, suspended between lust and that sharp bite of pain, and terrified he would stop.

He prepared her slowly. The pleasure became a tormenting surge of sensations as his fingers gently prepared her anus. There was no impatience, as Jase had often shown, no irritation that it took so long to prepare her. Beneath his unhurried caresses she eased, relaxed, until he was working three long fingers in and out of the back passage as her strangled moans echoed around the room.

"Yes, baby," he crooned into the dripping folds of her pussy. "So sweet and tight, Ella."

She moaned in protest as his fingers pulled free, then moaned again in rising pleasure as his tongue began circling her clit. She was unaware of his hands for long moments, unaware that more was coming. Her dazed senses only knew his hard breaths between her thighs, his stroking tongue…

Chapter Eight

"James…" She wailed his name as the head of the butt plug seared her anus as he pushed it into the tight entrance.

She fought the restraints, pressed harder into his licking tongue and nearly came to the smooth, stroking movements as fire lanced through her rectum. Thickly lubricated, the plug invaded her slowly, stretching her, burning her, bringing her so close to orgasm she had to bite her lip to keep from screaming out for it.

"James, please." She couldn't stop the strangled plea tearing from her throat as the anal plug lodged inside her anus, her muscles clenching on it, her pussy shuddering in reaction to the pleasure/pain.

He moved then, despite her protesting cry, pulling himself from beneath her thighs and kneeling behind her. Her hips arched to him, her body desperate, mindless. His hand landed on the upturned cheek of her ass in a surprisingly sharp blow.

Ella stilled. At first, shock arced through her body, then an excitement that had her stilling in fear. She didn't like it, she assured herself. It was depraved, perverted. She wouldn't like it.

"From now on, if you need to get off, Ella, you come to me. No more vibrators unless I insert them. Do you understand me?"

"James…" She shook her head, needing to protest, yet unable to.

His hand landed on the opposite cheek of her ass. She flinched, her body shuddering at the heat. She wouldn't like this, she promised herself again, though her pussy convulsed in nearing orgasm.

Then she felt the plug, seated so snugly in her rear, begin to swell. Slowly stretching her, burning her as his fingers went to her dripping vagina. One slid slowly inside her, caressing the thin muscle that separated her vagina from her anus. She could feel the enlargement of the plug as he caressed her there. The steady growth, the burning pain, the striking pleasure that shot through her body like flares of lightning.

"The plug enlarges, Ella, to eight and a half inches and several inches around. Almost as thick, almost as long, as my cock." She was struggling for breath when the swelling stopped. "Seven inches is all you can take now. When you can take it all, Ella, then I'll fuck you there."

Ella writhed against the blankets, fighting to accept the thickness of the device that stretched her anus. She could feel the heat steaming from her pussy, the sensitivity of her body, the agonizing need that was as much pain as it was pleasure.

"Here, baby." He was beside her then. Ella opened her eyes, staring up at him as he helped her to lever herself up as far as the chains he had loosened would allow.

She trembled, knowing what he wanted, more than eager to give it to him. She licked her lips slowly then allowed his cock to push slowly between them. He was thick and hard, so hot and demanding she moaned in exquisite anticipation as she closed her lips tightly around him and suckled slowly at his flesh. He burrowed in, sliding over her tongue until he was almost gagging her, poised at the entrance to her throat.

He stopped, breathing roughly as his hand wrapped around the flesh where her lips were closed around it. Then his hips began to move. She heard his groan as her tongue licked at him, her mouth sucking him as he began to fuck her with smooth, powerful strokes. She was restrained, at his mercy, a receptacle for whatever he commanded. She was helpless. She was insane with lust.

She suckled his cock with moist, noisy appreciation. There was no shame in the sounds she made, no trepidation that he would give her more than she could take. At least, not in this instance. There was only the hot male taste of him. Only the need to make him as crazy to come as she was.

"Damn, even your mouth is tight," he groaned as he fucked her slowly. "Hot and tight, Ella. But your pussy's going to be hotter, tighter. Like fucking a virgin with that butt plug filling your ass, tightening your cunt."

She trembled as his wicked words washed over her, but she suckled his cock like a woman starved for a man. She licked beneath the head, slurped at it, starved for the taste of his seed. The shaft throbbed, pulsed, but he held onto his control as she slowly lost hers.

"Enough," he growled long moments later as he pulled back from her.

Ella moaned in protest, struggling against the restraints, as she tried to follow the burgeoning erection. His hand landed on the curve of her ass again. A warning slap that only made her pussy vibrate with increased need.

"I've got to fuck you, Ella. I'll strangle you if I try to take my pleasure in your mouth now."

Ella stilled. Her breath rasped from her throat, fear suddenly trembling through her with almost the same force as her lust did. His cock was large, thick. The plug in her anus had tightened her vagina, and it had been more than a decade since anything larger than her small vibrator had invaded the channel. He would kill her with his cock…

"Not like this, I want to watch you take me, Ella." She was too weak to fight him as he released the restraints on her ankles and her wrists.

He turned her over on her back, then replaced them carefully. Ella stared up at him, unable to protest, unable to fight him. She ached in ways she could have never imagined. Her pussy felt as though it was boiling with heat, and the fullness in her anus only called attention to the emptiness of her vagina.

He leaned over her, his expression so gentle, so filled with approval that her heart clenched. When his lips covered hers, her womb flexed with melting desire. His kiss was hot, heated, tasting of her intimate juices and his male need. She moaned into his lips, wishing she could hold him to her, touch him, as she felt his cock nudge against the sensitive opening of her vagina.

"Ella," he groaned her name, his hand touching her damp hair, the other holding her hip as the head of his cock invaded her tight opening.

"Oh God! James!" Her head tossed as he began to push slowly inside.

"Easy, Ella. It's okay, baby. You can take me." She struggled against the restraints, crying out as he separated the sensitive muscles, powering through the drenched, fisted grip of her pussy.

She bucked beneath him, barely aware of her sharp cries of pleasure...or were they of pain? Her movements drove him deeper inside her. Deeper. Deeper. Her hips arched to him as he slid in to the hilt, the pulse and throb of the heavy veins beneath his hard flesh echoing through her body.

"Damn you, Ella," he cursed her, his voice rough as he fought for control. "You're so fucking tight I could come now. Look what you've denied us all these years. All these years, Ella, you stole this from us."

She screamed then. She had sworn she would never scream for him. But when he began the hard driving rhythm inside her tight clasp, the pleasure/pain that tore through her body pushed the desperate scream from her throat. She was bound to the bed, unable to fight the sensations, helpless against the rocking strokes that tore past her muscles, made her accept her own desires, the pain and the pleasure and the need for more.

Too many years longing. Too many nights dreaming. On the third stroke Ella exploded. The orgasm that tore through her body had her tightening further, screaming out his name, her body shaking, tensing, convulsing as she fought the strength of her release. But she couldn't fight it. Couldn't escape the hard, quickening strokes of his cock as he fucked her through the cataclysm, then a last desperate lunge as his seed jetted hot and harsh inside her convulsing pussy.

"Ella." He cried out her name as his lips buried at her neck.

She felt his release spilling inside her, her own rushing through her quaking vagina as her soul rocked with the pleasure, and she knew the emotions she had fought for so many years.

Her vision dimmed as she lost her breath with the last wave of intense sensation. Tears fell from her eyes, and as she collapsed back on the bed, she knew in her soul she would never be the same again.

Chapter Nine

"Hey, Ella, you missed dinner. Are you in there?" Ella jerked awake at the sound of her friend's voice that evening, her shocked eyes going to the bedside clock. Damn, she had forgotten about Charlie having the key to the house, and her habit of just coming in as she pleased.

It was dark, a little after ten, and James was still in the bed with her. Even worse, his half erect cock was still buried in her pussy where it had been after her last climax.

She moved to jerk away, but his arm around her hips stopped her, and her heart raced as his cock began to harden inside her.

"In a minute, Charlie," she called out, pushing at his arm. "I fell asleep. I'm sorry. I'll be out in a minute."

"Well, hurry," Charlie called back. "It's getting late and I need to head home."

The sound of the other woman's footsteps fading away from the bedroom door eased her harsh breathing until she felt James thrust inside the tight grip of her vagina as his throttled groan sounded at her ear.

"I have to get up," she whispered, pulling at his arm, wanting nothing better than to push back against him, to scream out in pleasure again.

"Damn," he muttered, though there was no anger in his tone, only regret.

Ella bit her lip as the hot length of flesh eased from her and he rolled lazily to his back as he reached over and flipped on the light at his side of the bed. She looked back at him as she wrapped the blanket around her and rose to her feet. He was naked and unashamed of it. His long fingers scratched at his chest as he smothered a drowsy yawn. His erection lay against his lower stomach, glistening with her juices and his earlier release. He looked sexy as hell.

Ella shook her head before he could tempt her any further, grabbed her robe and rushed to the bathroom. It took longer than she would have liked to clean the evidence of their spent passion from her body. Thankfully, James had removed the butt plug earlier, though her vagina and her tender back entrance were still a little sensitive.

Ten minutes later, she left the bathroom, covered in her long gown and robe. James still lay on the bed, watching her through narrowed eyes.

"She doesn't know you're here," she whispered.

His eyes narrowed further. "Who does know?"

She licked her lips nervously. "Just Tess and Cole."

"I see." His tone of voice suggested he might see more than she was actually saying. "So you want me to stay put?"

She shrugged.

Hell yes, she did. Her friends rarely kept secrets. What Charlie knew, Terrie would know, and Marey would know and Tamera. She winced at the thought.

She especially didn't want Tamera to know.

"Fine." He shrugged, though she didn't trust his tone of voice. "Go visit your friend. I'll be here when you're done."

He closed his eyes. Ella breathed in deeply in relief before she rushed from the room.

"It's about time. What were you doing in there, anyway?" Charlie turned from the refrigerator as Ella moved into the kitchen.

Charlie was nearly five years younger than Ella, slim and sophisticated, dressed in a gray silk sheath with matching heels. Her long, black hair fell to the middle of her shoulders like a fall of midnight silk, contrasting to the perfect peaches and cream perfection of her bare shoulders.

"I was asleep." Ella went to the coffee maker and started a fresh brew of coffee.

"You're never asleep before midnight, Ella," Charlie scoffed. "Hell, you're still up at one and two in the morning. I know, I can see your bedroom light from my house."

Ella lowered her head. She was unaware Charlie kept such a close eye on her. It was disconcerting.

"Sometimes I take a nap." She shrugged, flipping the switch and listening to the machine hum as it heated the water. "It's no big deal."

She turned back to her friend, aware of Charlie's steady regard as she took a slice of cheesecake from the refrigerator and moved to the table after grabbing a fork from the drawer.

"What's going on? You're acting strange." Charlie was the most perceptive of her friends, but Ella didn't like how easily even she was reading her.

"Nothing's going on." Ella took two cups from the cabinet and set cream and sugar on the table. "I was just tired, Charlie."

She was just damned uncomfortable now. Her thighs were weak and tender, her breasts marked by James' mouth, her body longing to return to him. She usually enjoyed her friend's visits, and looked forward to them. Charlie was easy going and often filled with laughter, but now Ella just wanted her to leave. She wanted to return to James; his heat, his hard body.

"Ella, you aren't acting right, honey." Charlie watched her with sharp, deep blue eyes. "What's going on?"

"Nothing." Ella shook her head as she poured the coffee. She had to fight the trembling of her hands, and the knowledge that everything was suddenly out of control. And not just sexually.

She set Charlie's coffee cup in front of her, then moved to the other side of the table and sat down. As she looked up, her stomach dropped. Charlie was staring across the room in complete shock. Ella's head turned slowly, knowing what held her rapt attention. Her brows snapped into a frown as James walked barefoot through the kitchen.

"You didn't tell me you were fixing coffee, baby." He wore blue jeans and nothing else. And those damned jeans. The top button was loose, and the waistband rode low on his tight abdomen. Right above it was a strawberry love bite. She remembered marking him, and now her face flamed as she realized her friend couldn't miss it.

"Dear God," Charlie breathed as she obviously fought for breath, her gaze swinging from Ella to James.

Ella could only cover her face as James poured his coffee, dropped a quick kiss to the top of her head and said, "I'll finish up some of that paperwork you dragged me away from earlier while you talk to your friend."

She peeked through her fingers as he ambled away. The jeans molded his buttocks to perfection, and Charlie wasn't missing a second of the view as he left the room.

As he disappeared through the doorway, Charlie turned to her, her eyes wide, her expression shocked.

"James Wyman," she breathed out in shock. "Oh my God! Ella, you fucked James Wyman? Or is it Jesse?" she squeaked in fear, well aware of Tess's interlude with Jesse Wyman and Cole.

Ella squirmed in her chair. No, she thought, he had fucked her, thoroughly. And more than once. She sighed tiredly. Everyone would know it now.

"It's not Jesse," she groaned, pushing her fingers restlessly through her hair. "You should know better than that."

"James!" she squealed.

"Dammit, Charlie, shut up," she shushed her frantically. "He'll hear you."

"Ella, do you have any idea what you're doing? What you're getting into?" Her voice lowered. "Honey, he and Jesse have shared their women more than once..."

"Not me." Ella came out of her chair, her hands trembling violently as she shoved them into the pockets of her robe.

"Maybe not with Jesse, but Ella, James and Jesse aren't the only members of their pack, hon. I could name half a dozen now."

Ella shook her head. "What the hell are you talking about?"

Charlie sat back in her chair, her mouth falling open in surprise. "You haven't heard? They're called the Trojans, babe. Because of their dominance, and their sharing. They like submissives, Ella. You aren't a submissive. Are you?"

"You know I'm not," Ella bit out. But she wondered. What James had done to her last night, the dark promises he had made to her as he buried his cock inside her over and over again, threatened her belief that she wasn't.

"Ella, those men, they don't mess with women who aren't submissive. Women who won't give them that ultimate commitment." Charlie came to her feet, facing her in concern. "You ran from Jase because of his demands. James will be worse."

Ella shook her head. "I'm in control," she whispered. "He won't do it if I don't want it."

"And when he leaves because you can't do it?" she whispered fiercely. "Dammit, Ella, haven't you been hurt enough?"

"It's my choice, Charlie." She raised her head in determination. "My choice. No matter what happens."

Charlie watched her silently.

"He's the one," she finally said slowly. "The one that came in while Jase had you tied down. The reason you divorced him and moved so damned far away for so long."

Ella turned away, her lips opening as she fought to drag in more air, to stem the panic rising in her chest.

"Stop, Charlie," she whispered, turning back to her as she stared at her friend pleadingly. "Please, let it go."

"My God. You're in love with him." Charlie shook her head, amazement shaping her expression. "Ella, he's the one. The reason you ran and turned into a bitter old nun. My God. He's younger than you are."

"Six years…"

"He shares his women," she pointed out again.

"I don't have to agree…"

"But you will to keep him." Charlie was angry now. Her voice throbbed with it, her face flushing with it. "You will, Ella. Because you love him."

"Enough." Her hand sliced through the air as her soul trembled with the knowledge. "This isn't any of your business, Charlie…"

"The hell it isn't." Charlie's voice rose with anger. "Dammit, Ella, I watched you destroy yourself after that divorce. Turning into a bitter old woman before your time because of that bastard…"

"Lower your voice." Ella was shaking with her own anger now. "And remember, Charlie, I didn't ask you for your opinion then or now."

"Like you have to ask for it," Charlie snorted in disgust. "Really, Ella. It's voluntary, darling." The sarcasm was a clear sign that Charlie was rapidly losing her temper. Ella wasn't far behind.

"Everything okay?" Ella's head swung around to the doorway and she wanted to groan in dismay when she saw James standing there, watching them mockingly.

"Don't you know how to dress?" she bit out in irritation, seeing all the smooth, perfect muscle that she knew Charlie was eating up with her eyes.

He arched a dark brow questioningly. "I thought all good little boy toys went around half naked? Don't tell me you're firing me after only a few hours on the job."

Chapter Ten

It was well after midnight before Charlie left. After James's mocking statement and his declaration that he was going to bed to let them discuss him in peace, Ella broke out the wine. Some nights, there was nothing you could do but get a shade tipsy and remember all the reasons why you didn't want a man in your life. Charlie was eager to go along with her. Evidently all that smooth male muscle and blatant sexuality had been too much for her to deal with at one time as well.

Finally, her friend weaved her way to the limo waiting on her, thanked her aging driver nicely as he opened the door for her, and crawled into the vehicle. Ella felt she herself was walking reasonably straight until she closed the door and turned around. She proceeded to walk into the embroidered chair that sat off to the side. She frowned down at it in irritation before backing up and trying again.

She needed to go to bed. But James was in her bed. She stopped as she headed through the kitchen. Of course James was in her bed. That was where he belonged, she decided with a sharp, rather jerky nod before squaring her shoulders and heading to the room.

He was waiting on her.

How had she known he would still be awake and waiting on her? His expression was cool, arrogant, as she removed her robe and started to lie down.

"The gown." His voice was dark, foreboding.

Ella stopped, staring at him in surprise.

"Excuse me?" she asked him haughtily. "I sleep in my gown."

"Take it off or I'll tear it off." There was no mercy in his voice, no change in his expression.

Ella snorted. "Some boy toy you are, James. I might have to fire you after all. You are supposed to obey me, not the other way around."

"Take the gown off. I won't tell you again, Ella." Her insides trembled at the dark brew of anger and desire that throbbed in his voice.

She did as he said, suddenly too nervous not to. She watched him helplessly as the silk gown slithered to the floor, leaving her bare before his eyes. What did he see, she wondered? She was older; her body wasn't as toned, as pretty as it had been ten years before. She knew all her problem areas, had stared at them in the mirror more times than she could count.

He pulled the blankets back and patted the bed beside him. Watching him warily, she got into bed, lying on her back as he stopped her from turning on her side. His big hand moved to her stomach, caressing the flesh there as her breath caught in her throat.

"I won't be relegated to the bedroom, hidden, a secret you keep from everyone," he warned her coldly as he stared down at her. "Do you understand me, Ella?"

"What do you want from me?" She shook her head, her brain clouded with the alcohol, her emotions sensitized from her friend's warnings, and James's demands. "Why are you even here, James? In my bed. My life," she sighed wearily.

"You have to figure that one out on your own," he growled, his hand moving until he could brush back the lingering strands of hair that clung to her cheek, her neck. "You should have already figured it out, Ella, but you refuse to look beyond your own fears. I won't allow that to continue."

His eyes softened only marginally as she stared up at him. In the soft light of the lamp, his features were shadowed, savage yet softening with tenderness. She lifted her hand until she could touch his beard-shadowed jaw, loving the warmth and roughness of his flesh.

"I dreamed of you," she whispered bleakly. "For so many years, I dreamed of you, James. You'll break my heart if I let you. I can't let you."

His gaze became shuttered. "Go to sleep, Ella. We'll talk tomorrow."

He moved then, turning out the light before lying down beside her, wrapping his arms around her as he pulled her close. Ella stared up at the dark ceiling, feeling the warmth and vitality of his body as he held her. Feeling the hard length of his cock against her thigh.

She breathed out regretfully. "I'll miss you when you're gone, James."

"Go to sleep, Ella," he warned, his voice soft yet commanding. "You don't want to push me much further tonight."

"But I will, James." She shook her head, the wistful sadness inside her heart too much to bear. "I was used to being alone."

Silence met her words. He wasn't asleep; his body was too tight, too tense for her to believe that. His anger thickened the air in the room, though, and she realized she didn't really want him angry. Keeping him angry was to keep him at arm's length, a safe distance from making her body torment her with its needs. But he was close now, he had already taken her, more than once, and the little aches in her body proved that.

"I used to fantasize about you." She frowned as she thought of the years that had passed. "How silly is that? That's when what little satisfaction I had found with Jase in all those years was gone. The moment you stepped into that room destroyed it all."

His cock jerked against her thigh.

"I warned you, Ella. I won't warn you again." She shivered at the dominating tone of his voice.

She turned her head to look at him, seeing only the shadowed impression of his form beside her. Her eyes lowered as she wondered what it would be like to see him out of control. All that cool purpose burned away. Could she do it? Could she make James Wyman, master of women, lose control? Her pussy gushed with the thought. She had heard rumors for years. Women talked, and unfortunately she heard the tales. And they talked about James and his cool control, his sexual deliberation. None had broken that calm. None had made him lose control.

She rolled on her side slowly, shivering as she felt him adjust his erection to her new position. His body tightened further.

"Maybe having a boy toy would be nice." She smoothed her hand up his chest, her nails glancing his hard male nipple as she scratched lightly over it.

He caught her hand, holding it still against his chest as he stared at her through the darkness.

"Do you think I'd make a good toy, Ella?" he asked her, his voice silky, dangerous. "It could blow up in your hands, sweetheart. You don't want to continue on that course."

She was just tipsy enough to smile. To lean forward and swirl her tongue over the sensitive nub of his nipple. She heard his breath catch, felt his body tighten further.

"Isn't that the point?" she asked him as she moved lower, her tongue stroking down his hard abdomen as the muscles there clenched tightly.

His hands threaded through her hair, clenching on the strands as she nipped at his flesh, trying to halt her movements. Ella couldn't halt her gasp. The prickling heat in her scalp was more exciting then she wanted to admit.

"Ella." He spoke her name sharply, a demand, a command to stop, warning her in the sheer dangerous throb that lingered in the tone.

"What, James?" she asked him softly. Her head held still just below his heart, but her hands were free. She raked her nails up his thighs, loving the sound of his breath catching in his throat.

"You don't want me to lose control," he warned her softly.

"Of course I don't," she whispered, her teeth nipping at his skin as her nails ran alongside his bulging cock.

It was exhilarating, exciting. He was breathing harder now, his heart racing beneath her ear. She tugged at the grip on her hair, whimpering with the stimulation, that sharp flare of pleasure that raced through her body. Her head lowered until her tongue was able to reach the flared, hot crown of his cock. He jerked as she licked it.

The grip he had on her hair was fierce, the burning along her scalp intense, but it only fired her body as a distant amazement pierced her brain. The pain was a fiery cascade of sensations that nearly broke her. She was out of control. She, who had kept her control wrapped about her like a mantle of protection, had fallen as easily to this man as a virgin with no knowledge of the heartache awaiting her.

She pulled further against his grip, crying out as she felt her cunt clench at the ache. Her lips capped the turgid head of his erection, slurping noisily as her tongue licked, stroked. She wanted him deep within her mouth, wanted to feel him fucking into it, unable to halt his own spiraling pleasure. To destroy his control as he had destroyed hers.

One hand gripped the thick shaft as his hips jerked, burying the smooth crown in her suckling mouth. She heard his strangled moan above her, felt his erection throb with a deep, hard flex of the tightened muscle.

"Enough." His voice was thicker now as he pulled at her hair. When that didn't help, he gripped her head, pulling her up as she cried in protest.

He flipped her to her back, jerking the blankets off the bed as he came over her.

"You don't want this, Ella," he bit out fiercely. "You don't want to tempt me this way."

She undulated beneath him, raking her hard-tipped breasts against his chest, rubbing her aching pussy against the thigh wedged between her legs.

"What will you do, James?" she asked him, tempting him, tempting fate and the dark visions suddenly rushing through her head. "How will you punish me? Will you share me then, to show me my place? To regain your control?"

He stilled. His hands held her wrists to the mattress as he stared down at her, his savage expression only barely discernible. He was breathing hard and fast now, fighting to regain the upper hand, and now she knew how to make him lose it.

"Can you bear it, James?" she asked him softly. "Will you join in, or merely watch as another man takes me, making me scream as you do, fucking me like you do…"

Before she could anticipate him, his control broke. His legs wedged between her thighs and his cock pushed inside her swollen pussy in one hard, long stroke. She screamed out at the invasion, at the instant, fiery pleasure.

"Do you know what you're tempting, Ella?" he groaned as she fought to accept the heavy girth buried in her cunt. "Do you know what you're doing to me?"

He wasn't still. His hips moved, his cock thrusting in and out of her in long smooth strokes as he fought to hold back. She didn't want him to hold back. She didn't want to hold back. Not any longer.

"How will you do it, James? How can you make me accept it? I dare you to try."

She didn't expect the consequences of those words. His lips slammed down on hers, slanting across hers as his tongue drove deep into her mouth. At the same time, the thrusts of his cock inside her vagina increased in strength and power.

Ella cried into the kiss, her tongue tangling with his as she tilted her hips to take him deeper, harder inside her sensitive cunt. She could feel her muscles gripping him, the thickness, the heat of his erection thrusting past the sensitive tissue, stroking nerve endings already enflamed with a lust she had never thought herself capable of.

And with each stroke, each demanding invasion into the core of her body, she was reminded of what caused his loss of control. The thought of her with him and with another. Two cocks, hard and strong, pushing into her over and over again…

Her body tightened, her cunt clamping down on the pistoning power of his cock as she exploded to the images twisting through her mind, her body. She tried to scream, but her mouth with filled with James. She tried to buck him away from her, to escape the driving pleasure, the knowledge, but her pussy was filled with James. Filled with him until he groaned hard and deep, powered into her one last brutal thrust before he exploded.

The wash of his hot seed inside her channel triggered another, smaller climax as she whimpered beneath him. Her body shuddered, her womb rippling with the orgasm as the ice that had once encased her heart shattered.

She loved James Wyman. And Ella knew to the farthest depths of her soul, that the love filling her would be her ultimate destruction.

Chapter Eleven

"I'll be back in three hours."

Ella lay face down on the bed at noon the next day, breathing through the fiery fullness that invaded her anus.

James had taken her again when they woke up. He had been quiet, almost reflective as they showered and ate breakfast. Later they had lain around the pool until having a light lunch that he had prepared himself. They hadn't talked much, but the silence hadn't been uncomfortable.

Ella had been wary, though. He wasn't pushing her, for anything. He was contemplative as though his loss of control the night before bothered him in some way. An hour after lunch he laid out the box that contained a mild anal douche and ordered her to use it. His voice had hardened, sending heat streaking through her pussy.

"So what am I supposed to do for three hours?" She turned her head, watching him with narrowed eyes.

Preparing her for the anal invasion had left her hot, wet. She wanted him now, before he left.

"Wait on me." His voice brooked no refusal. "Leave the plug in. I've removed the inflator, so you can dress, do what you normally do. Just do it as it eases the muscles there."

He had inflated it farther than before. Through a tormenting hour of heated touches, burning strokes of his tongue in and out of her pussy, but never enough to push her over the edge. She was burning with lust now and reluctant to move. The thick intruder buried in her anus stretched the muscles there with fiery precision. He had given her all she could take, yet had assured her that it still had not been fully inflated.

"Oh, that's fair…" She stopped. The look in his eyes was almost frightening. She settled back on the bed, watching as his brooding look eased only slightly.

"You pushed last night, Ella. You may think you've gotten away with it, but you haven't. When I get back, I'll show you just how you haven't. If you get yourself off, I'll punish you. I'll tie you down to this bed and leave you there for the remainder of the night, and I'll make sure you know how painful arousal can really be."

She trembled at the sound of his voice. She had no doubt he would do it, too. If she was restrained, there would be no tempting his control, no pushing his personal limits. He could torment her as long as he liked. He had proved that in the last hour.

He released the restraints that held her, leaving the chains attached to the bed as he moved away from her.

"Wear a dress. Something loose and light. When I get back, we'll see how much control you have, baby."

Something about those words had trepidation skittering through her body. She eased up slowly on the bed, feeling her pussy clench, drench further as the plug bit at her tender anal muscles. She stared up at him silently, watching as his eyes darkened, his body tensing at the sight of her swollen, hard-tipped breasts, and the arousal that she knew was obvious in her expression.

"What are you going to do, James?" she asked him softly.

"You know, Ella." He pushed his hands into the pockets of his slacks as he watched her, his voice throbbing with an emotion she didn't want to name. "I've waited ten years, and in those years you've refused to take my desire for you, or my needs seriously, let alone your own. Tonight, you will take those needs seriously. You'll take me seriously."

Had she ever seen him look so powerful, so commanding? Suddenly, she felt much younger than him, and definitely much less experienced. His command of his own power, his own control, went beyond age or experience, and entered that unknown realm of supreme self-confidence. He knew what he was doing, she realized suddenly.

James had a plan, just as he always had, she knew now. But why and what that the plan was, she couldn't decide.

"No other men." She shook her head, her hand trembling as she pushed her fingers through her hair. "I mean it, James. No one else."

His lips quirked. "You no longer set your own limits, Ella. I do. You'll learn that tonight. Whatever I want, however I want it, and you'll love it. Or you can continue to be a coward and deny what I know you feel for me. If that's the case, my bags are packed. Set them on the porch and I'll never bother you again."

She stared up at him, fear suddenly shaking her soul. "So I'm part of an orgy or I'm nothing to you, period?" she asked him, feeling her heart thunder in her chest. But what really terrified her was the clench of arousal that rippled through her cunt.

"No, Ella. I would never put you in the middle of an orgy," he promised her smoothly. "What I will put you in the middle of is more pleasure than you've known could exist. Pleasure I know you want. Need. Even now, after the past three days, you aren't satisfied. You climax until you nearly pass out with the pleasure of it, but you need more. And, by God, tonight I'll make sure you have what you need, or I won't bother trying anymore. I love you, Ella. Love you until my heart breaks with it, but I won't beg you, and I won't let you deny either of our needs. Now think about that."

Shock exploded through her body as he turned and left the room. She could feel her face paling, her body weakening at a knowledge he had possessed, and yet she hadn't.

It made sense now. James wasn't a man to chase after any woman, to care one way or the other if his desires weren't returned. Yet, he had chased her for ten years. Not in an obvious, lovesick manner, but in his own controlled, brooding way. He had made her aware of her own body, her own desires, even as she tried to hide from them, and made her more than aware of him.

She bit her lip, staring at the door, remembering his driving demands, his loss of control the night before. No other woman had managed that. Had it happened, she would have known about it. And his need for her wasn't diminishing. Like hers, it seemed to be growing stronger.

Even after the excesses of the past days, the fiery heat and lust that flared between them. He was right, she had kept reaching for more. Something, some unknown dark desire, kept pushing her.

She shook her head, fighting the awakening realization. For years she had fought Jase, not because she secretly wanted what he offered, but because he didn't satisfy her. He didn't bring her to the mindless orgasms James could bring her to. He didn't make her pussy drench with a look. His needs hadn't filled her with this strange excitement and nervousness. She had never wanted to break the control he thought he had.

She eased from the bed and walked slowly to the shower. A cool shower. She needed to think, she needed to make sense of the past and of the present. But more than anything, she had to decide if the desires that filled James were truly a part of her own needs, or just a part of her desperation to keep him now that she had held him. She had to know, before she took the chance of losing him forever.

Chapter Twelve

"I need to talk to you." Of the five friends Ella had kept over the years, Terrie was perhaps the freest; the one Ella felt would be the most likely to understand her present predicament.

Silence met her request for long minutes. "Charlie called this morning, too," Terrie finally said softly. "Are you okay?"

Ella closed her eyes.

Of course Charlie had called. Terrie, and Marey and most likely Tamera as well. Just what she needed, everyone to know who and what she was doing. Her parents would know, too, if they were still alive. Poor Charlie, she couldn't keep anything from their small group of friends, no matter how hard she tried.

"I'm fine," she finally whispered. "I just need to talk."

"I'll be right over, then." She could almost hear Terrie's sharp nod.

Ella hung up the phone, sighing deeply. Terrie would know James the best. She had been married to one of his two brothers, the bastard. Ella, for one, was glad to see his final demise. Thomas Wyman had been a stone cold prick.

As she waited for the other woman to arrive, Ella made sweet iced tea, moved about the kitchen preparing glasses and fought to ignore the heat in her rear. The plug was driving her crazy. Her panties were damned near drenched from the moist heat of her pussy and no matter what she did her nipples wouldn't soften and just go the hell away. The scrape of the light cotton fabric of her sundress over them was about to drive her to distraction.

It wasn't long before she heard the front door open then close, and Terrie's voice calling out her name from the hall.

"I'm in the kitchen." For as long as Ella could remember, the kitchen was the favored spot for her and her friends to talk, to argue, to visit. Either over coffee or sweet tea, it was there they seemed to find the most comfort.

She set the glasses of ice and the pitcher of tea on the table as Terrie swept into the room. She stopped inside the doorway, looking around curiously. "Is the boy toy in residence today?"

Ella winced at the question, though it could have been the tight, erotic tugging of the plug in her rear as she sat down, she thought.

"James went somewhere," she sighed. "He didn't say where."

"He's meeting Jesse for a drink." Terrie shrugged as she sat down across from her. "Jesse was supposed to come over to the house and fix the faucet for me but James had some kind of emergency."

Ella watched her friend suspiciously. "Are you sleeping with him?"

"James?" Terrie's eyes widened in surprise.

"No, not James," she bit out. "Jesse. I know you're not sleeping with James, you would have killed him by now."

Terrie poured the glasses of tea and slid one closer to Ella. "Jesse isn't like James, Ella."

Ella lifted her brows at that surprising statement. "Have you lost your mind, Terrie?" she asked her carefully. "I caught him with Cole and Tessa. You are aware of this, right?"

"Well, Ella, you were so drunk that night when you called us over that you couldn't keep it to yourself," Terrie sighed regretfully. "I am aware that he likes to play. But he's not all dominant and fierce like Cole and James are. Jesse's softer."

Ella snorted. Terrie hadn't seen Jesse, her beloved brother-in-law, that day as he lay beneath Tess, obviously spurting his release inside her. The man was just as dominant as his brother. He just hid it from Terrie. The reasons he would do so worried Ella. Terrie didn't need more heartbreak, or more pain.

"I'm not here to talk about Jesse, anyway," Terrie reminded her. "We're here to talk about you and James."

Ella was smart enough to recognize the same denial tactics she had used herself with James. She sighed wearily. Maybe Terrie was the wrong friend to call.

Maybe Jesse was the wrong brother to call. Unfortunately, James thought, he was his only brother. Even when Thomas had been alive, Jesse was still the only brother he had to talk to. The only other person he trusted.

"I love her, Jesse. What if she won't accept it?" James couldn't get the thought out of his mind.

His sexuality was a part of him, a part he didn't want to change, and saw no reason to change. Could he have been so wrong about Ella? Was he mistaking the excitement, the unspoken challenge she tempted him with? Could he do without watching another man fuck her? He could, it wasn't about sharing her. Besides, it wouldn't be a common thing. He wasn't that depraved. He wanted his woman to himself. And only one man. He had already discussed it with the one he had chosen to introduce her into the pleasures of a threesome. But could she accept it?

James was well aware that Charlie had, in depth, given Ella all the gossip she thought she had on the Trojans. He snorted silently. The ninny who had pinned that name on them didn't have the sense God gave a goose. Unfortunately, one of the leading members of the unofficial group had married her. He sighed wearily.

Whatever name you put to it, they were a group, of sorts. Nearly a dozen men who had met in college, and over the course of several years had gravitated together based on their sexual practices and their need to discuss and learn from each other's mistakes. There had been many. Often due to a member's unlucky choice of a lover who refused or even reviled their dominance. At present, there were eight of them, all in their thirties, all still looking for that one woman who could accept them.

Jesse leaned back in his chair, tipping back his beer and taking a healthy drink as James watched him. Finally, he shrugged. "She most likely knows what's coming, James. Ella can be a pure witch when she's riled. If she hasn't cut your balls off yet, then most likely she's not going to."

James winced. That didn't do much to reassure him. He sipped his own beer, staring up at the ceiling of Jesse's home as he contemplated the coming evening. He had called Saxen earlier to set the time to meet him at Ella's home, and as that time rapidly approached, he found he was becoming more nervous than he had thought he would be.

"Saxen was my choice for tonight," he informed his brother quietly. Jesse nodded slowly. "He's a good choice."

The tall, dark-skinned engineer worked with them at Delacourte Electronics as well, and was one of the most dependable men James knew.

He had spent over an hour talking to Jesse and getting nowhere. He wasn't any closer to stilling the nerves running riot inside him than he was to begin with.

"You have been of absolutely no help whatsoever," he finally sighed as he set the empty bottle on the glass coffee table and rose to his feet to leave. "Remind me of this when you finally decide to get off your ass and make your move on Terrie."

Jesse grunted as he rose to his feet to his feet. "Damned women. What did we do to deserve them?"

James shook his head. "I would say we were just lucky, but I'm starting to wonder about that one."

Chapter Thirteen

His bags weren't sitting on the porch. James pulled in behind Saxen's Mustang and breathed out a hard sigh of relief. He'd be damned, but he had never been this nervous in his life. His entire future, his relationship with Ella, and his own needs were riding on this final day. If she turned him away, would he have the strength to stay in control and to walk away from one of the most important aspects of his sexuality?

He would if he had to. He admitted that to himself. Ella was more important than his desire, more important than his life. But he knew if he allowed it to happen, then neither of them would ever know complete fulfillment. That was his main concern. He knew Ella, better sometimes than she knew herself, and he knew she needed the extreme boundaries of sex just as intensely as he needed them for her. Pulling the keys from the ignition, he opened the door and stepped out of the car as Sax unfolded his tall frame from the other car.

"You need a bigger car, Sax." James repeated the comment he made every time he watched the other man slide from the low-slung car.

"James, that's my baby," Sax grinned, his teeth flashing white against his dark skin as he ran his hand over his slick, shaved head.

The sleek, little blue car was indeed one of his prized possessions, though he could have afforded better. That and the Harley. Sax had a set number of priorities. He had achieved all but one. Poor Sax had his eye set on a woman that wasn't about to let him anywhere near her. She would make his life hell, James knew.

"She might throw us out of the house." James paused at the bottom of the steps as he glanced at Sax. "She might shoot us."

Sax chuckled. "If you're brave enough to go after this one, James, then she should be brave enough to accept you. You've gotten this far without frostbite. I bet you last through the night."

Ella's nickname, The Ice Queen, had followed her even after her divorce to Jase.

"Frostbite?" James murmured as he shook his head. "That's the least of our worries, Sax."

He opened the door and stepped inside. He had left explicit instructions for her in the letter he had left in the living room before he went to Jesse's. He had been careful not to voice those instructions for fear of her outright rejection. If she didn't want this, then the luggage on the porch would have been a more humane way to cut his heart from his chest. Of course, a bullet would be more permanent.

"She should be in her room," he murmured. "Either restrained to the bed or waiting with the gun."

Sax chuckled behind him, and in the sound James could feel the other man's excitement. Sax was one of the few men who hadn't known Ella during her marriage to Jase. He had wanted his partner in this next experience with Ella to be free of any preconceived notions or ideas of loyalty. Ella was his. Sax would continue to join in periodic threesomes with him and Ella if this first session went as James hoped.

Just as Jesse would continue with Cole and Tess until he took that final step in securing his own woman. After marriage, there was no need, no desire to touch another woman. The commitment was strong, the need so extreme that other women held no attraction. It was often a confusing, hotly debated issue among the men who shared in this lifestyle. The need to see their women experiencing that pleasure of an added element to their sexuality. The periodic addition of another man, and in one case he knew of, another woman.

He stopped at Ella's bedroom door, took a deep breath, and opened it slowly as Sax leaned against the doorframe. God help him. He nearly came in his slacks. She had buckled the straps to her ankles as he ordered, and her arm into one of the wrist restraints. She was staring at the ceiling, her breathing hard and rough as he walked slowly into the room.

He moved to the free wrist restraint and bent over to buckle it slowly. He caressed her wrist, feeling the hard throb of blood in the vein beneath her skin. She gazed up at him, a shade of fear mixing with the excitement in her gaze.

"Are you sure, Ella?" He sat on the side of the bed, cupping her cheek gently as he stared down at her.

She was trembling. He could feel the fear and excitement traveling through her. It would heighten the sensations, he knew; make the arousal, the coming orgasm more intense, hotter and brighter. He could barely hold back his own anticipation. He had waited, longed for this more years than he could count.

"No." She breathed out roughly. "I'm not sure of anything right now, James. Don't ask me questions like that."

His lips quirked into a soft, gentle smile. Despite her words, he could see that she was more than ready. Her breasts were swollen, her nipples hard little points atop the firm mounds.

"You'll only be restrained until we think you're ready to be released," he promised her softly as he stood by the bed and began to undress.

The word "we" had a small, strangled whimper escaping her throat. He watched the shiver that worked over her body, the way her nipples tightened, hardened further.

"Is the plug still inside you?" he asked her gently as he dropped his shirt to the floor, aware that Sax was slowly undressing behind him.

"No." Her voice was low, breathless. "You told me to take it out."

"You followed my directions exactly?" He kept his voice firm, stern.

Her eyes were wide, dark as she watched him, careful not to look toward his hips. Nervousness and excitement had her body quivering on a finely balanced edge of desire and lust.

"Exactly." Her voice trembled.

He stripped off his pants and boxers, his hand going to the near-to-bursting erection that stood out from his body. He was so damned hard he knew he wouldn't make it five minutes if he didn't find relief soon. A relief he knew her sweet, suckling mouth would provide him.

"Sax, loosen the chains on the footboard. I need her sweet mouth first, or I won't make it."

"I don't blame you. She's beautiful, James." Sax spoke for the first time as he moved to the bed, his own cock thick and hard as he stared down at Ella.

Her gaze flickered to him, her eyes widening as they caught the sight of his cock, as hard and long as James's, if not a bit more so. Her gaze flew up to him and he could see the fear in her eyes.

"I'm scared," she whispered, her hands curling into fists as he sat down beside her on the bed again.

"The fear is good, to a point, Ella," he told her gently. "You have to trust me, though. You have to trust that I won't allow you to be harmed, that I will never threaten you, never cause you undue pain in any way. Without that trust, baby, we're wasting our time here."

His hand reached out to cup one of her full breasts, his fingers gripping the nipple firmly. She breathed in roughly, the little point tightening further. Leaning to her he drew one of the hard points into his mouth, relishing the thick moan that vibrated at her throat.

When his head rose, he was pleased to see the flush of lust, of deepening desire coloring her once pale face.

"I love you, Ella," he said softly. "Above all things, I love you."

She nodded her head sharply. "Fine. Fine." She was breathing hard and deep, then her eyes widened, shock flaring in her expression as her gaze went between her thighs.

James followed her look and his lips quirked into a smile. Sax couldn't resist soft, wet pussy, and he was lapping at the creamy mound now with the intent concentration of a man enjoying a prized dessert.

He couldn't help but watch, and Sax gave a show worthy of any porn star as he made certain each touch, each stroke could be clearly seen. His tongue ran through the narrow slit, parting it, gathering the thick juices on the tip of it before he licked them into his mouth and started again. Slow, teasing strokes of his tongue that circled her pink pearl clit then returned to her tender opening to start all over again.

Then his fingers parted her, his dark flesh an erotic contrast to her pale skin. When he had her lips flared open, his tongue distended then disappeared slowly inside her vagina. James' cock jerked at the sight of it, imagining the feel of her pussy gripping the other man's tongue, her muscles rippling around it as he fucked in and out of the hot channel.

"James." He saw her hips jerk, the muscles of her abdomen tightening as her body tensed, her legs moving against the restraints.

Sax was slurping on her now, sucking as much of the thick honey from between her thighs that he could reach. And James knew even more would replace it. It would be impossible to suck that well of sweetness dry.

"Shhh." James leaned forward, his tongue licking over her lips as she stared up at him with dark, shocked eyes. "Just enjoy, Ella. Just enjoy."

He kissed her. A long, wet kiss that had her moaning into his lips, her head lifting from the pillow as she fought to get closer. Sax's noisy feast below seemed to make the kiss more desperate, heated, as her body began to clamor for release. A release she would be screaming for before it ever came.

His lips moved from hers, his own breathing rough, impatient, as they traveled down her neck, moving unerringly to the hard-tipped breasts that rose and fell roughly. She was moaning, her head thrashing on the pillow as she fought to get closer to the mouths tormenting her.

Sax would tease her. He wouldn't want her release coming until she was sandwiched between them, any more than James did. And she would be ready for them. Then he heard her shocked gasp, the moan of near pain that erupted from her throat and knew Sax was preparing her back entrance as he stroked her cunt hotter.

"It's okay, baby." He kissed her nipple, licking it gently as he rose to his knees beside her. "Just enjoy, Ella. Just let it feel good."

He gripped his cock in his hand, grimacing at the near black of her eyes, the flush of lust on her face. She was so beautiful it was damned near killing him.

"James, I can't stand it." She bucked against Sax's mouth as James looked to the other man.

Sax had pulled back, watching as two of his fingers sank slowly in her pussy, two up the forbidden depths of her anus. Her heels were pressed into the mattress, fighting for leverage to thrust against the shallow thrusts. Sax wasn't about to hurry, though. He knew as well as James did, the pleasure she would experience from the teasing.

Sax's head lowered again then, unable to keep his lips, his tongue, from the soaked slit that flowered open for him. He murmured his enjoyment into her flesh, his eyes closing as he savored each lick. James felt his cock drip with his own pre-cum at the sight. Her moans, her ragged breaths, the unconscious sexuality reflecting in her face, in her jerky movements, was more than he could bear. If he didn't push his swollen cock into her mouth soon he was going to go insane.

Chapter Fourteen

Ella wanted to scream, to find some way to release the surging sensations building in her body, but she couldn't find the breath. Seconds later the choice was taken out of her hands as James' cock slipped past her lips, filling her mouth, as his rough groan echoed around her.

Her lips tightened on him, her tongue licking over the thick veins, the tight flesh in greedy hunger, as the scents and sounds of sexual need wrapped around her. The flared head of his erection sank nearly to her throat as her tongue worked desperately along the shaft. She suckled him, pulling her head back then pushing forward, tempting him to fuck her mouth, to spill the hot rich seed that tasted like nectar on her tongue.

Between her thighs, Sax was lapping at her cunt, his tongue dipping into her vagina, two large fingers sliding deep inside her anus. She shuddered with the sensation, moaning around the flesh thrusting between her lips as she fought to suckle it, to tempt him into the release she knew he was teetering on the edge of.

She was suspended on a rack of agonizing pleasure and desperate fear. She had seen the other man's cock, thick and hard, the dark flesh appearing angry, eager to take her. How would she bear it? How would her body hold two thick shafts like that at the same time?

"Ella, you're killing me." James's voice was thick and deep as his hand gripped the halfway point of his cock and his thrusts became harder. "Your mouth is so sweet, so hot."

She felt the head pulse against her tongue as she delved beneath it to the sensitive spot that she knew would make him groan with dark lust. The sound shot to her womb, ripping through her with almost climactic intensity. She tightened her mouth on him, slurping on his hard flesh hungrily as his thrusts became harder, his breathing rougher.

He was on the edge of release, she could feel it, almost taste it, but she was as well, and the tormentor between her thighs was refusing to send her over. She strained against his suckling mouth, his piercing tongue, but nothing seemed to be enough.

She growled around James's cock as she fought for that one stroke, that one caress, that would send her over the edge.

"Stay still." A sudden, light slap to her mound as the other man moved back had her stilling in surprise.

Her eyes flew to James's face as he watched her, then glanced down once again.

"Again." James's voice was soft. "She's not sucking me properly, Sax. I think she needs to be punished for it."

Her mouth was full of James's cock, but her strangled scream should have been enough. When the lightly stinging blow landed, she felt her entire body flinch. Not from pain, but from shameful pleasure. Her clit throbbed, pulsed, so swollen and sensitive now that the light blow was agony and ecstasy all in one.

Her mouth tightened on James's cock, her tongue stroking, her mouth suckling as she knew he liked it, but she was determined that when the restraints came off, so did her façade of submission. This was all well and good, but she would make certain they both paid for the tormenting arousal.

Another blow landed. She jerked, moaning in protest at the streaking sensations. Her clit swelled further, throbbing in an agony of arousal. When the next blow came, she growled around the cock thrusting into her mouth and raised her hips for more. More. One more blow aimed just right, and her clit would explode.

But the next smack never came. Instead his tongue stroked, caressed, running around her clit with light, deliberately teasing strokes. She rewarded James, the beast, with a firmer suction on his erection, driving him past his own control.

"Yes, Ella. Baby. I'm going to come now. Take me, Ella." He powered in, his moan deep and hard as his cock suddenly exploded.

Thick and hot, his seed shot into her mouth as his body jerked with the pleasure she knew was washing over him. In return, the mouth on her cunt only teased her more. She continued to suckle James's flesh, drawing the last drop of his tangy seed from the tip as she fought to keep from screaming out in agony.

"Perfect." James pulled back from her, his cock still hard, leaving her mouth reluctantly.

Perspiration coated his body. His eyes were dark, his face flushed, his lips heavy with sensuality as his hands went to her breasts once again.

"Are you ready, baby?" His hands went to the restraints at her wrists as Sax moved away from her to loosen those at her ankles.

Ella shuddered. Her pussy was on fire, desperate, yearning. Every nerve ending in her body was sensitized and throbbing for release. When they released her, Sax moved to the side of the bed, laying back, the bulging length of his heavily veined cock rising to his abdomen. As she watched, he rolled a condom over the throbbing shaft, preparing to take her.

Ella moved, coming quickly to her knees as she caught James's shoulders, her hands moving to his head as she pressed her lips to his. The surprising action seemed to fray his hard-won control. His tongue plunged into her mouth as she felt them moving her.

They lifted her over Sax's big body until she felt the wide, flared head of his cock nudging at her vagina. She pulled back then, staring up at James, seeing the heady excitement in his gaze as the other man clasped her hips, holding her still.

"I'll take you anally first," he whispered. "Then Sax will take you. Scream for me, Ella. Don't worry about control, don't worry about anything. Just the pleasure."

She groaned as Sax drew her down to him, his lips whispering over her cheek, her neck, as he drew her head to his hard shoulder. Below, his cock throbbed at the opening of her cunt.

"Relax, Ella," Sax's voice was soft, soothing. "It's like nothing else you'll ever experience. Nothing else you'll ever know."

She flinched as she felt two fingers, slick and cool, slide into the prepared depths of her anus. She cried out, pressing closer, desperate to drive the hard cock inside her pussy as James tormented her back entrance.

"Stay still, Ella." Sax's fingers tightened at her hips. "Patience, beautiful. Patience." Then James moved into position. She felt the head of his cock nudge against the little puckered hole a second before he began to press inside. She tried to arch, but Sax held her close and still. Her wail, one of agonizing arousal and the sharp bite of erotic pain, was muffled against the shoulder beneath her as James entered her with excruciating slowness.

"James," she cried out his name as Sax's hands held her still, closer, his cock throbbing at the portal of her cunt.

She felt the burning stretch of tight muscles, heard James groan, praising the heat and the grip of her tight channel. One hand gripped a buttock, flexing, tightening on her as he surged inside her last few inches with a hard, shockingly deep groan.

Impaled, stretched and overfilled, Ella fought to breathe through the first fiery thrust, then to adjust to the invasion. She tightened on his cock, her breaths beseeching cries as her cunt flooded with moisture, convulsed and fought for release.

"Now," James groaned behind her. "Now, Sax, I won't last long."

"Please." She felt the condom-covered tip of his cock force its way into the entrance of her pussy.

She bucked against them, the heat and hardness searing her, the pleasure/pain more than she could bear as he worked his cock inside her by slow degrees.

She tried to thrash in their arms, tried to force Sax to enter her faster, harder, dying for the orgasm she knew was just out of reach.

"James. Damn. She's tight." He groaned beneath her as he rocked inside her, the slick inner juice easing his way, but not by much.

As each agonizing inch pressed into her cunt, she could feel James, thicker, harder, as he throbbed inside her ass.

"Almost there," Sax groaned. "Hold on, baby, I'm giving it all to you."

She screamed, loud and deep, as the last inches powered inside her with a strong surge of his hips, burying his erection into her to the hilt. A second later, James began to move behind her.

The sounds of wet sex, desperate cries and hard male groans filled the air as Ella shuddered, her body jerking almost spasmodically in the grip of a lust she could have never imagined. The two men, their thrusts perfectly timed, began to fuck her with hard, driving strokes. Her inner muscles protested, flared with heat, but parted beneath the driving strokes of the two thick shafts possessing her.

Between them, Ella cried out their names repeatedly, pushing herself into each thrust, flying higher, surging deeper into the ecstatic orgasm she knew was building faster, harder inside her.

Their thrusts quickened then, pushing into her body with rapid movements, rasping her clit against the wiry roughness of Sax's pubic hair until the moment insanity hit. She felt her mind, her heart, her womb and her pussy explode. Convulsively, simultaneously, as her scream rocked the air between them. Behind her, James stiffened at that moment, his hot seed flooding her anus as Sax thrust into her tightening pussy one last time and tightened, his groan of release sounding hard and loud at her ear.

"Ella, baby." James leaned over her, holding her close as she continued to cry out, her body shuddering so harshly she feared she would break apart.

"James," she cried out his name, tears wetting her face as another vibration wracked her body, tightening her, blinding her. She tightened on the cocks still filling her, riding her through the mindless orgasm until she collapsed, boneless, against Sax's body.

"Ella. God. Baby." James pulled her from Sax, easing her into his arms as he fell to the bed, holding her close, tight, as the other man got up.

Ella could still feel the internal shudders racing through her womb, her own release dripping from her cunt as James rocked her, his lips caressing her face, his hands stroking her back.

"Don't leave me." She burrowed closer against his chest, too exhausted to hold him to her, praying he would hold her to him instead.

"Never," he whispered at her ear, his vow echoing to her soul. "Never, Ella. I'll always be here."

Chapter Fifteen

"She asleep?" Sax was waiting in the kitchen, dressed, looking smartly presentable. He didn't look as though he spent the last hours helping James fuck Ella into another screaming climax. James had held her in his arms, stroking her body, easing her through the destructive shudders of her orgasm before moving to take her again himself.

After the first violent sensations had eased from her body, neither man had been able to leave her in peace. She responded to each touch, each stroke of their hands, as though it were the first time.

"She's asleep." James replied, wishing he were as well. He had never been so exhausted in his life.

"Will she be okay?" Sax glanced back at the hallway that led to her bedroom, a frown shaping his brow.

"She'll be fine." James was sure of that. Her sleepily muttered words as she finally gave into her own exhaustion assured him of it.

"Well, you waited long enough for her." Sax rolled his broad shoulders as he headed for the hallway. "I'm heading home now. I need to sleep."

James followed him to the door and as the other man turned back to him, lifted a brow questioningly.

"I'll need your help now," Sax said with a fierce frown. "You and Cole set up Ella's downfall. I expect your help setting up my woman's fall."

James grinned. "You have a deal, Sax. Give me a chance to figure out how to get to her, and I'll let you know."

Sax nodded. "I'll be waiting. Impatiently, but waiting."

He walked out the front door, closing it softly behind him. James sighed deeply, secured the locks and then returned to Ella's bedroom.

She was in the same position he had left her in, curled up on her side, her auburn hair a cloud of silk around her face, her expression peaceful, serene. Had he ever seen her peaceful or serene before he invaded her life? He shook his head, knowing he hadn't.

"Is he gone?" she mumbled as he eased into the bed beside her.

Surprised, James stared down at her closed eyes.

"He's gone." He pulled her into his arms, tucking the blankets around her again.

Her voice was drowsy, replete, as she snuggled against him. "No more threesomes." She yawned. "I can't move."

He chuckled gently. "Let me know when you need to move and I'll do it for you," he assured her.

Silence thickened around them again for long seconds.

"What now?" she asked, her voice even, though he heard the worry in her tone.

"Hmm. Many things." He smiled against her hair. "But I'm not leaving, Ella. Not now, not ever. You're mine. You submitted to it, baby. You can't back out now."

The letter he had left that day was detailed in more than one regard. Submit now, submit for life. The ring that had accompanied it graced her finger, just where it belonged.

"You have a lousy way of proposing, James. I'm going to have to teach you better. Boy toys are supposed to be more romantic, especially married ones." Warmth filled her voice, a warmth that gave him hope. Then joy swelled in his chest when she whispered, "Especially the one I love."

He laughed then, feeling freer, happier than he could ever remember feeling.

"I'll keep that in mind, baby." He kissed her lips tenderly, feeling her smile, her exhausted response. "Sleep now. In my arms, Ella. The way it's supposed to be."

And they both slept.

Epilogue

He had sworn she would come to him. He wouldn't spend agonizing months trying to ease her into a relationship she had stated she would never tolerate. So he tried to seduce her into it instead.

After Thomas's death, he had made himself indispensable to her. He was at the house often, fixing this or that, just talking or watching movies late into the night. Despite appearances, Terrie was a wary person, well aware of how easily she could be hurt, how weak she was physically. From what he had gathered, his brother had been more of a bastard than he had ever imagined.

"Now that was a beautiful wedding." Terrie stumbled against him a bit as he helped her into the house.

James and Ella's wedding ceremony had made her teary eyed, reflective. She had sat in the limo on the way home, quiet, a bit sad, staring out the window as her fingers stroked over the upper swell of one breast that her cream-colored dress had revealed. The action had caused his cock to swell, to harden in agonized need.

"Well, it wasn't a long one, anyway." Jesse pulled her to him, leading her to the living room, enjoying her soft weight against his side.

The soft silk of her dress slid against his hands, and when he sat her on the couch, the hem rode just below the crotch of her panties. Cream-colored as well, silk. He was betting it was a thong.

"You kissed the bride." Her comment had his brows lifting.

He had kissed the bride. Long and deep, to her complete surprise and shocked arousal.

"Yeah, I did." He knelt at her feet, removing the high-heeled shoes from her small feet.

"That was so decadent," she bit out. "Kissing her that way, with your tongue. You made her horny."

He smothered his laughter. "That was the point," he whispered up at her as he caressed the slight welts on the side of her foot.

She pouted. She had such an intriguing pout and used it on him often.

"I promise not to kiss Ella again." His hand stroked her calf as he felt a small tremor work over her body.

"Sax fucked her. He was at the wedding, of course," she bit out. "I knew she couldn't hold out. She gave in too easily."

She sounded angry with Ella, though Jesse knew she was more than happy that her friend had finally found some happiness.

"You, of course, would be much harder to convince?" he asked her, careful to keep his voice even, his hand on her calf comforting rather than arousing.

She leveled a hard look at him. "I am not so easy."

That was sure as hell the truth. He murmured consoling words, though, massaging her foot, well aware of how the heels made her feet ache.

"I'm not your sister." She jerked her foot from his grasp, staring down at him angrily. "Stop treating me like one."

"Keep it up and I'll turn you over my knee and paddle your ass." He jerked her foot back. "Now what has you so upset? I thought you were happy for Ella."

"I am." She was pouting again, watching him darkly.

"Then what's your problem?" he asked her again.

"You've never kissed me like that," she finally bit out, her cheeks blooming with a flush. "Why haven't you?"

He pursed his lips. Her breasts were moving quickly beneath her dress, her nipples hard, poking impatiently at the light fabric. He allowed his hand to stroke higher along the inside of her leg.

"Because," he whispered. "I can never decide where to put my tongue first."

She blinked, confusion filling her expression. "What?" Her question was almost a gasp.

"You heard me." His hand stroked to her thigh. "Do I take your lips and plunge my tongue into your mouth, Terrie, or do I push it as deep and as hard up your pussy as I can, and suck all that sweet cream into my mouth? Deciding is a bitch."

Her mouth opened, her thighs tensed. He watched as she fought to breathe, to draw in air to counter the arousal he saw surging in her gaze. He parted her thighs then, his cock jerking at the sight of the damp spot on the silk of her panties. His gaze rose back to hers.

"Do you want that, Terrie? My mouth buried in your cunt, my tongue fucking you to orgasm?" Her thighs opened farther as a strangled moan whispered past her throat.

"Please," she whispered, and his cock surged in joy then throbbed in disappointment as he gently closed her thighs.

"Remind me when you're sober, Terrie." He stood to his feet, staring down at her shocked expression. "I won't fuck you drunk. Sober up, then call me. But don't be surprised if you find out exactly why Sax was at that wedding and what he's most likely doing right now to your friend's climaxing body. You won't play with me, Terrie," he warned her softly.

He turned and left the room, then the house. If he didn't, he knew he would fuck her, knew he would drive his cock so deep and hard inside her she would scream for her orgasm. And he couldn't. Not yet. She hadn't seduced him; she didn't want it enough. When she did, well then, he grinned, then he would give her everything he had ever dreamed she could take.